Conversations

I0548269

With a

Married Woman

And The Humorous Tale of Becoming One

By

John Kincaid

**And the two shall become one flesh
Mark 10:8**

**Breathe in the moment,
Exhale the memories.**

Conversations With a Married Woman
And the Humorous Tale of Becoming One

Introduction

Do you know what other couples say to each other in the privacy of their own homes or while driving down the road on vacation? Do you know what they say while eating breakfast or walking along a county lane? I bet you don't. Well, neither do I. Have you ever wanted to pull back the curtain and eavesdrop? I bet you have. Well, here is your opportunity. I *do* know what my wife, Janie, and I talk about, and I am willing to share some of that information with you. I think you are in for a treat.

I am going to pull back the curtain and share with you some of the conversations we have had. My intention is not to reveal any great secrets about marital communication or wisdom about interpersonal relationships or bonding or intimacy or any of those other noble topics. My intention is not to impress you with what a perfect couple we are. We are not. No. My intention is simply to entertain you. I am not an expert on marriage or marriage communication. I have no idea how other couples communicate or relate with each other. I do not know anything about bonding or intimacy. I only know how Janie and I relate to each other. I know how we have bonded. I do not pretend to have any rules of engagement, no hints, no tips on conflict resolution. Anything I may say along those lines are just rules that work for me and Janie. So, please do not take this as a model of how couples should build their relationships. What we do works for us. It probably will not work for you. So just be prepared to be entertained, not enlightened. If, however, you pick up a wisdom nugget or two along the way that can be applied to your marriage, all I can say is "You're welcome."

I am reminded of one famous couple, George Burns and Gracie Allen. You know George Burns was God, and Gracie was by far his better half. They were comedians whose act consisted of comical banter between a husband and wife. Burns played the straight man. Allen played a silly, addle-headed woman, but often in her innocence got the upper hand in the conversation-and most of the laughs, often times making George look foolish. They entertained audiences for decades. Well, Janie is no addle-headed woman, and our conversations will never reach the level of George and Gracie's banter. They were pros. We are mere amateurs. Their banter was scripted. Ours was spontaneously adlib. (I know. That is redundant.) They entertained audiences for decades. We are shooting for a just couple of hours. At the end of this book, I hope you say "Good read." Even a "Wow, these two are nuts." will suffice.

Janie and I have been married for over fifty years. It does not seem that long. This little book is a compilation of some of our mostly humorous conversations and life adventures. The adventures are ancient history. Many of the conversations are recent. At my age, anything within the last ten years is recent, except what happened last weekend, which I can barely remember. These conversations are presented in no particular order but do paint a mosaic of our life together. These are all real, spontaneous conversations and events involving a wise, no nonsense, sharp-witted realist-Janie-who will love you like a pit bull (I will explain later.) and someone who is just trying to keep up-me. I hope you enjoy these exchanges as much as we did. Along the way, you may accidently learn a point or two about marriage. Maybe not, but at least I hope you have a good laugh or two.

Before presenting the conversations, I will start with some background material, some ancient history if you will on how we met and got married. That may sound boring, but trust me, I think you will enjoy it. For the record, Janie has read and "approved" everything I am saying, even though she thinks my memory on certain points is suspect. Thus, this is the authorized version.

The One-Eyed Back Alley Bridge Player

It all started over fifty years ago in the late 60's at the Bear's Den at West Virginia Institute of Technology. The Bear's Den was the student union where everyone met to have a snack, study or just hang out between classes.

For my freshman year in college, I had attended a small, boring, expensive institution in Kentucky. For my sophomore year, I decided to transfer back to my home state of West Virginia and enroll at West Virginia Tech to give my dad's wallet a break. Being only fifteen miles from my parents' house made traveling home much easier and faster. As a freshman, I had hitchhiked on several occasions some two-hundred miles to get home. Yes, I was foolish-and cheap.

Anyway, at the start of my sophomore year, I was just minding my own business in the Bear's Den when I glanced up at the staircase coming down from the upper level. And there she was. Her long hair hung over one eye, and her miniskirt revealed slim legs suitable for a movie star. She impressed me as the most attractive woman I had ever seen-even if she only had one eye. I was immediately smitten. The Beatles song *Got to Get You Into My Life* started playing in my head. I had to meet this beauty. I had to know who she was. I am not sure who subsequently introduced us, but I am eternally grateful.

Timeout. I know some of you are shaking your head right now and saying, "Wow, this guy is treating this girl as a sex object." Well, yeah, maybe. Biology works that way-initial physical attraction. Without it, most of us would never have been born. This initial physical attraction prompted me to want to know more about this mysterious one-eyed girl. I soon discovered there was more to her than long hair and great looking legs. And I did find out she actually had two eyes. For a while, I really thought she only had one and used her long hair to hide that flaw. In a way,

3

I felt sorry her, and that made her even more attractive to me. That I could actually be attracted to a one-eye girl taught me something about myself that I did not know, which was I could actually like a girl who was not perfect, and with one eye, this woman was not perfect. One day, however, she tossed her head to one side, her hair flew back over her shoulder and-voila! -her other eye was revealed. OK, I thought. I can still be attracted to a normal two-eyed girl.

I must say, however, this was more than just initial physical attraction. There was something that told me this was more than a good-looking woman. There was something special here, something of substance, and I needed to discover what that special something was. Yes, something of substance communicated via a miniskirt. The Lord works in mysterious ways. For the record, Janie claims her skirts were not too short, her legs were just too long.

I soon discovered she was, despite the short miniskirts, an upstanding, God-fearing, Church-of-God Girl with high standards and a no-nonsense attitude. How high were her standards? She was a beacon of sense and stability among students in the Age of Aquarius. She was raised and taught by her grandparents who lived through World War I, the Great Depression, and World War II. Because of that, she has told me on more than one occasion that her generation has much better morals than mine. She is an older woman but only by fifteen months, so timewise we are in the same generation, but her outlook was (and is) definitely old-school. Sometimes, I do believe she is a transplant from a bygone era, a lonesome soul caught up in a wayward time

4

warp eddy.

As I learned more about her home life, I discovered the core of her being was constructed on the principles of integrity and uncompromising commitment to values, love, loyalty, and devotion to family- a family that during her teenage years she was barely able to hold together. Her Hippy miniskirts were just a façade, folks. An attractive façade, but just that: a façade. Inside that eye-catching body dwelt a person of substance and wisdom beyond her age, which at the time was only twenty. The obstacles, disappointments, and challenges she had faced as she grew up was way beyond my experience as a pampered member of my extended family. I was impressed. I will write more about her family life later.

Her outlook and approach to life contradicted and yet strangely complimented my live-in-the-moment perspective. Apparently, we balanced each other out. These personality differences have led to a number of philosophical disagreements over the years, but they have been profitable disagreements for both of us. In essence, I toughened up and she mellowed out (a bit, just a bit). Her counterbalance to me was refreshing and attractive in and of itself.

I learned that her name was Janie, a simple, no-nonsense name, and I soon discovered that she played a mean version of Back Alley Bridge. She had an impeccable game strategy, and we seemed to communicate telepathically. We became an invincible duo, feared by the other bridge players. She was also smart and witty and well, frankly, she was hot, in a metaphorical sense, of course. What more could any young man want? We soon became partners playing Back Alley Bridge. Partners at bridge soon evolved into partners in dating, a whirlwind romance and marriage, and well, here we are together over fifty years later with four kids, eleven grandkids, two great grandkids, a cat, and an imaginary, second-reincarnated dog.

That First Christmas

Our first Christmas together was almost our last. In 5 B.C. (Before Children) when we were dating as sophomores, we visited Janie's father and stepmother in Kingwood, West Virginia. This was before interstates in the rugged mountain state, and I was too poor and cheap to own a map. On the way back to Charleston, I made a wrong turn, and we found ourselves somewhere in the middle the Monongahela National Forest-with a flat tire. This was before the days of cell phones, so I was stuck proving my manhood by changing the tire all by myself. I had never changed a tire before, but this was no time to ask for help from my relatively newfound girlfriend.

This made us late on our journey, and as we started descending the west side of the Appalachians, the early-evening sun disappeared into a snow storm. Lost, on our own, and still not sure if we were on the right road, we drove through the storm as the snow came down increasingly harder. Before long, the road was covered with ice and snow, but the snow kept pouring down.

"Do you know how to drive in snow like this?" Janie asked apprehensively.

"Oh, sure. I've done it lots of times."

I lied. To protect my status in her eyes, I lied. I had never driven in snow, but I had watched my dad do it a number of times. He seemed to be able to navigate slick roads effortlessly. Like father, like son, I thought. Driving in snow could not be hard to do. Silly me.

And then on that remote mountain road somewhere in the Monongahela National Forest as I drove through a curve, the car started sliding, spinning out of control, and was headed toward an icy precipice. (That is college-level talk for steep, snow-covered cliff.) I had no idea how to steer out of a slide. We were going to die on our very first road trip. I imagined we would lie at the bottom a ravine, undiscovered until the spring thaw months later. Our families would be in great agony and grief, not knowing if we were dead or just ran off to California together. Funny what runs through your mind when you are facing unexpected, sudden death.

While I struggled with my death fantasies and furiously attempted to regain control of the car, my cool, hip, sophisticated, metaphorically hot traveling companion was grasping my arm and screaming passionately, hysterically, "Oh, Johnny, Johnny, oh, Johnny!"

In that moment, I knew just by the way she was breathlessly screaming my name that I would be spending the rest of my life with her-even if it were for just a few more seconds.

Obviously, we did not drive off the cliff, but that watershed moment when fate revealed my destiny is indelibly etched in my memory. Janie says she was not being passionate; she was just stark-raving terrified.

New Year's Eve

I was at Janie's house on our First New Year's Eve. She lived with her grandfather about twenty miles from my house, and we both commuted to school. Her mother had died when she was born, and her father essentially abandoned her to her maternal grandparents. Her grandmother died when she was in high school and so, she lived with her grandfather whom she called "Dad." I called him Bill. For the record, he loved her more than anyone could love another person and sacrificed greatly for her sake. I saw from him where she got her strength.

Her grandparents tried to adopt her, but for some reason, her father would not let them. The courts forced her to occasionally spend time at her father's house. He was an executive for a coal company. He made big money, but never shared any of it with her. Janie speculated that it would reflect badly on him if he totally let her go for adoption. She dreaded the visits to her father. Both she and her Grandpa Bill were afraid the judge would take her away from her real home and make her live with her biological father. She had a half-sister and two half-brothers, but they have never been close. Grandpa Bill was the only family she had.

I found out a few years later how poorly she was treated by her father and stepmother. They never came to visit their grandkids, our kids. At Christmas time, we would get a call from her stepmother. She would tell us they were coming through the Charleston area to visit her relatives. She would inform us that if we would come meet them at the Kmart parking lot, she would give us our Christmas presents. That is the way they celebrated Christmas with us-a five-minute meeting at the Kmart parking lot on Patrick Street. And the gifts? Well, my kids will tell you they looked like clearance items from a thrift store, totally cheap with no thought given to them whatsoever. That is the unloving and insecure world in which Janie grew up.

8

And me? Well, I was the oldest of four siblings, and for years I was the oldest grandkid in a large extended family. Dad had two sisters and three brothers, and I was the center of their attention for about five years. In fact, they would "borrow" me from time to time to have a kid to play with. Seriously. One summer Aunt Lucille and Uncle Lawrence took me home with them for a month to live in Detroit. They had no children and wanted to "test drive" having a kid. Seriously. It was like heaven for me. I got a hot dog and root beer float almost every evening from the A&W down the street. I almost got to see the Lone Ranger in person, but he got drunk (so Uncle Lawrence told me) and did not show up for the event.

I guess my company suitably impressed Aunt Lucille and Uncle Lawrence. After that summer, they went on to have two kids. Denise and Robbie could thank me for my good behavior. If I had misbehaved, they probably would never have been born. Aunt Jo and Uncle Bradon did something similar with me the next summer. But no A&W floats from them. They lived in a "holler" in West Virginia where I learned to play in a creek that had icky runoff from a strip mine. I survived. I was also fortunate to have lived next door to my grandmother who "hugged me up" whenever she wanted.

Thus, I grew up in a loving, nurturing environment. I knew nothing about rejection or insecurity. But Janie did. I know now how much that influenced how she has lived her life. She has quietly, methodically, patiently, and deliberately constructed a family environment in which none of her offspring would go unloved or feel insecure.

But I digress. Back to our First New Year's Eve.

As I said, Janie lived with her Grandpa Bill some twenty miles from my house. The previous week I had wrecked my dad's car. I had fallen asleep coming home from a date and ran the car into a ditch on Deep Water Mountain. Fortunately, I veered left instead of right. Going right would have put me over a hundred-foot cliff and certain death. The car was scraped up but drivable. Still,

9

Dad grounded me from using it. I am not sure how I got to Janie's for New Year's; probably hitchhiked. So, it was just the three of us who celebrated our first New Year's Eve together. No fancy party. No elaborate celebrations. Just me, Grandpa Bill and my slim-legged and sometimes one-eye girlfriend.

After our "celebration," I had to go home. Grandpa Bill's rules. No overnight stays. I started out hitchhiking and made it a little over half way home. Around one o'clock in the morning, I became stuck at the foot of Deep Water Mountain. No cars were coming by, and those that did sped right on by my outstretched thumb. In those days, there was a serial killer on the loose in the region. He was known as the Mad Butcher. He preyed on hitchhikers, picking them up, killing them and then cutting them to pieces, stuffing them into duffle bags. The duffle bags were found on the side of the road. What I was doing that night was incredibly dangerous and stupid. Oh, and did I tell you it was snowing? Yeah, snow was coming down hard and heavy, furthering the decline in traffic. My options were growing bleak. How was I going to get home? My house was still another ten miles away.

Out of desperation, I started knocking on doors. If you have ever been in Deep Water, WV, you would know there are not a lot of doors to knock on in that little village. I finally found a house that would answer the door at one o'clock in the morning. Mercifully, they let me inside, and I made a long-distance-collect call home for help. My dad refused to come get me! He was obviously still mad at me for busting up his car. He was going to let me freeze to death or get hacked to death by some madman on the slopes of Deep Water Mountain. So, my options were freeze to death on Deep Water Mountain, get hacked to death by the Mad Butcher, or call my relatively newfound girlfriend for help. Embarrassing. Humiliating. So, so humiliating. But I was not above humiliation.

Fortunately, Janie and Grandpa Bill did not turn down my plea for help. They drove through the snowstorm and picked me up. However, they did not want to risk going over the mountain in such bad weather. Instead, we went back to her house, and Grandpa Bill made me sleep on the couch. Fine by me. I was just delighted to be out of the snow and out of the reach of the Mad Butcher.

The next morning when I was still on the couch, Janie came in and gave me a kiss good morning. Her soft hair brushed my cheek. She then went to the kitchen and started fixing breakfast. I could see her from the couch. Her hair was pulled up in pigtails. I had never seen her in pigtails. She looked really good in pigtails.

I had also never seen her without makeup and miniskirts, but she did not seem to care. She was dressed in a simple, cotton granny gown, but that did not matter. She was quaintly beautiful. I noticed that as she scrambled the eggs her body swayed ever so slightly. She took timeout from cooking to come back to the couch and gave me another kiss. This time her bacon-scented fingers gently stroked my cheek. Folks, do you know how sensual bacon-scented fingers can be?

Suddenly, another Beatles tune popped into my head. Quite frankly, folks, if it were not for the Beatles and rock music, we probably never would have gotten married. The words to the song drifted around in my mind, "Something in the way she moves, attracts me like no other lover." I was hooked, and I think she knew it. I am convinced that she knew from the start that those bacon-scented fingers would trip the snare.

And when she served up the bacon and eggs and coffee-in her simple robe-with no makeup-and unkept pigtails-and bacon scented fingers, I thought: "Yeah, I can do this every morning."

The Proposal

I never officially proposed to Janie, at least not in the traditional way. If I had knelt before her with ring in hand, and blabbered "Will you marry me?", she would have turned away giggling.

I think the "proposal" happened this way. We both commuted to school. She came in from the west. I came in from the south. Each morning we would meet at a coffee shop across the railroad tracks from the campus. By the second semester, we were both working in the computer center, so we had other opportunities not only to meet but also work together. Working together gives you a whole different insight into what a person is like. I found Janie to be a conscientious worker but relatively uneducated about computers. That was OK. Back in the late 60s, most of the engineering faculty was computer illiterate.

The computer center was a state-of-the-art facility. It housed one of the latest IBM business computers, an IBM model 1130, which had a memory of 8,192 16-bit words. By comparison, your average laptop has at least 1,000,000,000 bytes of memory. This was, indeed, a highly advanced computer-the size of an executive office desk. Laughable by today's standards, but a big deal back then.

Janie and I were computer operators, processing computer programs in the form of punched cards for faculty and students. Additionally, we were responsible for maintaining the computer in operating condition. In other words, we turned it off and on from time to time. We also processed the grades each semester and never once encountered a hanging chad.

Anyway, we would start the day off with coffee together at this little cafe. Even on a work-study budget, we could afford to do this. Coffee was about five cents a cup back then. This was before the days of all the Starbucks idol-worshiping of perverted coffee flavors and inflated prices. Personally, I believe anything added beyond a little cream and sugar is not really coffee.

Those morning meetings were magical. Her hair was all clean and shiny and sweet to smelled, sometimes pulled up in pony tails, sometimes hanging loose with her iconic one-eye look. I don't know what perfume she wore but just being in her presence was invigorating.

For the record, I now know her perfume brand. There is only one scent she has ever worn. Even today, men and women, even strangers, will come up to her and say, "I like your perfume." Some of the men will actually say, "You smell nice." Seriously. Do they not see me standing there? Do they think they can out Alpha-male me and steal my woman? Janie graciously humors them and says thanks, and they probably walk away with a warm-fuzzy feeling, grateful for her fleeting attention.

As I remember, one day on a cold January morning as we were sitting, sipping our coffee and refining our Back Alley Bridge strategy, *Judy in Disguise* was playing on the café's radio feed. It was not a Beatles song, but the group sounded a lot like the Fab Four. The music must have triggered a flash of genius in one of us and influenced the other to be receptive to the idea.

Suddenly, one of us blurted something like this. I am not sure who said this. Could have been me. Could have been Janie, but someone blurted out, "Hey, we could save a lot of money on coffee if we just got married. We could just brew our own at home. It would be a lot cheaper. Maybe we could even buy a couple of travel mugs."

"Hmmm," mused the other person in this conversation, "You know what? That sounds like a good idea. Let's do it."

It was all that simple. Just blame it on John Fred and his Playboy Band.

So, after that "romantic" proposal, we went shopping together to pick out a ring. It was a beautiful diamond one that cost a whopping $159. Big problem. I did not have $159. I had a whopping dollar and thirty-nine cents in my pocket. Thus, I had to buy Janie's wedding ring with an installment loan. Big problem. My credit was not good enough to qualify for an installment loan. Janie had to cosign for her own ring.

Embarrassing. Humiliating. So, so humiliating. But I was not above humiliation. We were in love.

Now that I think about it, since Janie was so eager to cosign for the ring, I think she was the one who had that fantastic idea for saving money on coffee.

Get Me to the "Church" on Time

Janie and I eloped. We had known each other for nine months. We were now both college juniors on work study making $1.25 an hour on a 20-hour work week. And then I nailed down a summer job doing computer programming for a major chemical company. I was making 520 bucks a month! Scientific programming was an emerging technology in 4 B.C., and I was quite good at it. I was so good that the professor assigned me the task of making up the tests for the FORTRAN class-a class I was taking. (Yes, I aced my own tests, but the professor failed them.)

Being young, naïve, and impatient, and with a sudden influx of big money, we decided to get married right away. Hey, we had been engaged for four, maybe five long months. We had no wedding plans, but what is better than "winging it?" Grandpa Bill owned a building with two apartments. These were luxury apartments-two tiny rooms, a kitchen the size of a microwave, and a micro-bath. Each apartment was probably 400 or 500 square feet, a little larger than a hotel room. But that was plenty of space for us.

So, we eloped. For various personal reasons, we eloped. One Friday, after getting my first $520 paycheck, we headed for Pearisburg, Virginia. We were told a judge down there would marry us. Remember, neither social media nor Google existed at that time to confirm this. Much to our chagrin when we arrived in Pearisburg, the judge told us the rules had changed. He could not marry us, but he did offer an alternative. He knew a judge friend in Chesterfield, South Carolina who would marry us, but we had to get to his house before 9:00PM to fill out an application. A 24-hour waiting period was required.

Encouraged by this, we headed south towards South Carolina. I owned a 1960 Renault. It was just a little larger than a motor cycle. and the engine was about the size of two loaves of bread. Oh, and it had a cracked engine block.

15

Consequently, we had to stop periodically to add water to the radiator. As we sped down Route 220, I would have to accelerate going up the rolling hills of North Carolina in order to coast back down the other side. Luckily, the engine lasted long enough to get us to Chesterfield.

We pulled into Chesterfield as the sun was setting. We had not eaten all day. This was 4 B.C. Fast food places were few and far between, especially in a small town like Chesterfield. We came upon a local ice cream shop, and looking at the time, we decided we had enough time to spare for a quick snack. And then I saw the sign: Sundaes Half Price. OK, I am cheap. I am of Scottish heritage. I did not have a lot of money, and credit cards did not exist for poor college students in 4 B.C. We hurriedly ate our cheap sundaes and rushed down the street to the judge's house.

They were nice people, the judge and his wife, and the judge did not question or challenge our desire to get married. As we were filling out the application, disaster struck. The Sundae sitting on an empty stomach combined with a case of nerves hit Janie's system full force. She ended up throwing up all over the judge's bathroom. I am sure then they thought Janie was pregnant and took pity on our plight, but she was not pregnant. For goodness' sake, this was 4 B.C. That is four years Before Children, but that did not keep the judge and his wife from believing that a child was on the way.

We finished the papers and set a time for us to come back the following night for the "ceremony." We found a little motel, the Magnolia Court, (Fifty years later, it is still there.) to stay the night and impatiently found things to occupy our time the next day until the appointed time for the marriage.

When the time came, Janie changed into her wedding gown in the judge's bathroom. She had no mom. She had no bridesmaids. She had no dad to give her away. We took no wedding pictures. There was no reception, no honeymoon cruise, nothing beyond the bare necessities for a wedding-two people in love. Yeah, that is an old-

16

fashioned notion, isn't it? When she came out of that bathroom in her wedding dress, she was the most radiant, beautiful, scared-out-her-wits bride I had ever seen. Note: This is not a picture of the wedding. This is a picture of Janie as a bridesmaid at a wedding for someone else, but this is as close as you are going to get for a wedding picture.

After the marriage vows and with all of the official documents in hand, we headed back toward West Virginia. We stopped for the night just south of Winston Salem. See the motel receipt on the next page. It was a real swank, upscale motel, fitting for our elopement, and the price was right.

The next morning, we hit the road early. The little Renault started acting up almost immediately. We would barely make it to the top of a hill and then coast down the other side. This method worked until we passed Mt. Airy (Andy Griffith's

Mt. Airy). We started up a long steep incline to Virginia on Route 52. Then, near a little roadside market selling cured hams, watermelons and cheap souvenirs, the Little Engine That Almost Could blew up. No attempts to revive it were successful. We were stuck. Stranded. Less than one day into our marriage, we were a family in crisis.

Remember folks, the last time I was stranded beside the road in a snow storm my dad refused to help me. On that occasion, I called my girlfriend, but I no longer had a girlfriend. I had a wife, and she was sitting, slumped beside me on the hood of the car in the sweltering July heat. My only option was to call dad.

Fortunately, mom accepted my collect call.

"Hi, Mom. I'm married. We need your help."

I do not remember what she said in reply. I am sure she was not surprised but not happy about that news. Frankly, she did not like Janie and did not approve of my marrying her. She preferred my former God-Fearin' Baptist girlfriend instead. I do not think it was anything theological. She just preferred Baptists. Overtime, however, Janie won her over with her Canasta card-playing skills, but out of the gate, well, the only direction their relationship could go was up.

Dad responded to our cries for help and brought his truck to tow us home. We were over a hundred miles away. We were relieved when he got there. He did not seem angry or irritated or anything like that. He calmly hooked up the towing bar to the dead Renault, and we started home. Just north of Bluefield, Dad had a flat tire.

All our early road trips were never without incident or excitement. The following year on our first trip to the beach, we drove through fierce lightning storms and flocks of bats. The next morning, I was busy digging dead bats out of the grill of the car. On a subsequent beach trip, Dad and I ended up sleeping on a park bench while Mom and a pregnant Janie slept in the car. Someone had failed to make hotel reservations. And then there was the time we got thrown out a McDonald's in Phoenix, and Janie got stranded in New York by a terrorist attack, and . . . oh wait, I digress.

So, I had a dead Renault, and Dad had a flat tire. No problem. Just put on the spare tire. Wait. Not that easy. Dad had thrown the wrong size spare tire in the back of the truck. The holes would not fit. The tire could not be mounted. Luckily, Dad was a mechanic and had lots of tools. With hammer and chisel, he managed to eventually widen one hole on the tire, enabling it to slip over the bolts on the axel and thus we hobbled home.

One thing you should know about my dad. He loved me. In that whole episode, he never became angry. He never said anything about the marriage. He never said anything about the broken-down Renault. He always treated Janie like a daughter, and he never brought the incident up. Never.

The next day, we bought Uncle Clarence's used Rambler for $100. It was only a notch better than the Renault, but it lasted long enough to get us through college. In only three days, we had made it through our first marriage crisis. And that, folks, is how I spent my first big paycheck.

That weekend in our new apartment, Janie decided to make a meatloaf. She had never used an electric stove, and it did not operate as she expected. Consequently, it took three days before the meatloaf was done. I began to question her cooking skills. I think she did, too.

Dad took the Renault and repaired the engine. He then cut the car in three pieces, threw away the middle piece that included the backseat, welded the front and rear pieces back together and made a riding lawn mowing out of it. Thus, it was a happy ending all around.

19

The Hunt

And now a politically incorrect, un-Woke poem about dating, at least dating the way it used to be.

She was slim as fence rail,
Sweet as a pie
And he vowed he would have her
If not, he would die.
"No love has been deeper,
Never more true,
And if robins have feathers,
Then I will have you."
But she fled like a field mouse,
"Oh, no!" she would cry
As she beckoned him onward
With a wink of her eye.
And so, he pursued her
Like fox chasing hen.
If he could but catch her,
Her love he would win.
From time immemorial
Gardens have grown,
Fields have been planted,
Seeds have been sown,
And boy has chased girl
For the wink in her eye
And long legs, and soft hair,
And kisses like pie.
But oft times the hunter
Ends up the prey
Like the love sick lad
On her grand wedding day.

The Great Swimming Pool Scandal

In our senior year, Janie and I decided to take swimming lessons at the college. Yes, college credit for swimming class. I needed another A to lock down my Magna Cum Laude rating. Janie needed the class to learn to swim.

On our first day in class, Janie and I walked into the pool area dressed in swim suits, of course. If you think a miniskirt was attention getting, try a black one-piece bathing suit. Very few women attended Tech in those days, and she was the only woman in the swim class. All the guys saw few women on campus and most of those females were more interested in business administration than boys. These guys were starved for female attention. As Janie and I walked in, all of them eagerly began ogling her, probably trying to come up with a clever pickup line. This was not the age of Woke or political correctness, folks. This was the late 60s and animal magnetism cloaked in a sophomoric New Age paradigm ruled the day.

I felt a little uncomfortable with all the attention these guys were paying my wife. I had to assert my Alpha-male dominance, so I quickly let everyone know we were married, i.e. "She's with me!" as Elton John would one day sing. The ogling quickly subsided and a number of the guys looked disappointed. Very disappointed. I just smiled and thought, "Sorry, guys. I found her first, and by the way, my clever pickup line was, 'Wanna play some cards?'"

And what was Janie's reaction to all the unwanted attention? Nothing. She was completely oblivious to it. She paid no attention at all to the admiring (and probably lustful) stares. Having come of age in the free-wheeling 60s, she was accustomed to it and knew that the best course of action in most cases was to shut them down with a cold shoulder. Yes, it was the 1960s, the dawning of the Age of Aquarius, the sexual revolution. All you Woke people, get

21

over it. That is the way it was-an era of free sex-except Janie was not handing out any free sex-at least not to them. She was a certified, strait-laced, no-nonsense Church-of-God-Girl and free sex was not on her radar. Thus, she was oblivious to their stares. Besides, she had a more immediate concern demanding her attention. She was genuinely petrified, deathly afraid of the water. She was also terrified of the one-meter board, and she refused to think about the three-meter.

The instructor proceeded to go over the class goals and grading requirements. He was going to teach us how to float and swim. He was going to teach us the various swimming strokes, doggy paddle, sidestroke, backstroke, breast stroke, freestyle, etc. For the final and only exam, everyone had to stay afloat for ten minutes. He did not care how—float, swim, levitate-as long as you avoided drowning. You just could not touch the sides or bottom of the pool or hang onto the diving board. We also had to dive off the one-meter and three-meter diving boards to begin the ten-minute test. Simple enough, I thought. No studying necessary. My Magna Cum Laude was a sure thing.

The instructor talked to each of us individually in order to determine our experience and skill level. Janie was a basket case. The instructor realized this and tried to be encouraging. After he heard her concerns, he looked her over, paying special attention to her two natural flotation devices, and then he made an awkward attempt to reassure her. Meanwhile, I was thinking, wow, this guy is not any better than our drooling classmates.

"Ma'am," he said, "you should have no problem floating. You have a lot of natural buoyancy there with your, ummmm, well, ummmm, you know," he said, as he motioned his hands toward her breasts. "I will have no problem teaching you to at least float."

Yes, he was standing right in front of me and talking with my wife about her breasts. But it was in a clinical/tutorial sort of way, so I guess it was alright. She was amused by it, and his breast compliment did keep her from bolting for the locker room in terror.

For the record, Janie was not offended by any of this. She found it amusing. I guarantee you, if she had been offended, she would not have been shy about letting people know. She is not a wallflower.

Well, this instructor was an absolute failure as a swim coach, and Janie's "natural buoyancy" was of little help. She panicked and sank to the bottom of the pool every time she got her face wet. Have you ever tried to swim without getting your face wet? She never got accustomed to having water in her face, thus failing completely with any and all swimming techniques.

And the diving boards? She left scratch marks on the underside of the one-meter where she had wrapped her toes around the end of the board in a desperate attempt to hold on. I think she fell off the one-meter once. That qualified as diving in the instructor's opinion. She never even made it up to the three-meter. He gave her a pass on that one.

When time for finals came, everyone joyfully jumped off the diving boards and then swam and/or floated in the water for ten minutes. Everyone except Janie. She could not navigate the driving boards. The instructor finally told her to get into the water using the steps, which she did with great trepidation. For ten minutes she clung to the side of the pool, continuously wiping water from her face, looking like she was about to be eaten by the Creature from the Black Lagoon. She managed to not drown, but she failed the test miserably.

Mercifully, the instructor did not fail her. I am convinced that if anyone else in the class had performed as Janie had on the swim test, they would have been given a failing grade. The instructor, however, allowed her to slip through because she was an attractive female. Whether we like it or not, there is a natural tendency for that kind of response. Instead of an F, he gave her a grade to match the size of her natural flotation devices-a C. He could not, however, accept his failure as an instructor. Shortly after the semester ended, he resigned in disgrace from the athletic department and ended up, I think, selling plastic toothpicks door-to-door.

Janie did manage to learn to play in the ocean, but she will not do the water rides at the amusement parks. Years later, in a foolish burst of courage, she went white water rafting on the New River. She survived. Barely. She said it was the closest she has ever been to Jesus in her life. I told her she really looks incredibly cute with a truly frightened look on her wet face. She was not offended.

For the record, the overt ogling of my wife at the pool was a bit of an eye opener for me, no pun intended. I had not realized until then how brazen men could be, and collectively brazen at that. Janie told me later that before we had ever met at least two professors had propositioned her-Age of Aquarius, free sex type of propositions. Being a good Church-of-God-Fearing, and Independent-Thinking West Virginia Girl, she naturally declined their offers. A couple of years later, our older-than-dirt landlord made similar advances in exchange for free rent. That was way over the line for both of us, and we moved out at the end of the month.

I remember how women were treated in the old sci-fi movies from the 1950s about radio-active monsters. Giant ants, rabbits, spiders, and all types of dinosaurs would be on the loose. The fate of the world was at stake. In most of the movies, a young, attractive female scientist would show up. She would be subjected to ogling, unwanted as well as wanted advances, suggestions that "we don't need a woman" in the group, "a woman will just slow us down" or "this is much too dangerous for a woman."

Instead of running to the HR department, she simply slipped into her high heel shoes, rolled up her sleeves, fixed her lipstick, and proved the men wrong by vanquishing the monster, much to their collective amazement.

The Value of Looks
Circa 2010

And now, let us fast forward a few decades to some random conversations with and stories about a married woman: Janie. These are presented in no particular order. Neither are they presented in any order of importance. You might consider it a kind of stream-of-consciousness dump. So, sit back and enjoy the ride.

Janie was reading the morning paper as we sat at the kitchen island eating breakfast. She started shaking her head.

"Look at this picture. Ya see that? This young girl was arrested for dealing in drugs."

"Yeah, too bad."

"It's such a shame," Janie lamented. "And she's so pretty."

"So," I said in a rare moment of insight, "would it be OK if she were ugly?"

Think about it. The world reacts differently when bad things happen to attractive people. "What a shame. What a tragedy," you will hear people say. In general, somehow that same empathy is not afforded to ugly people. "Just, look at this guy who got arrested. He looks like a scumbag. He probably got what was coming to him," most of us will say.

So, the next time you read a news story, do not look at the pictures. Remember, the sirens of ancient Greek mythology that lured sailors to their deaths were beautiful creatures.

During another conversation, I noted that Mick Jagger and the Rolling Stones were fortunate because they never had to worry about losing their looks.

Marriage 101
Cira 2000

I was teaching a class in church, comparing various religions. I was working on the Mormon faith and found something interesting to share with Janie.

"Did you know the Mormons believe you can be married for 'time and eternity'?"

"Really?" Janie replied.

"Yes, they believe you can be married forever."

"In heaven?"

"Yep. In heaven. For time and eternity. Forever."

She thought for a moment and finally concluded, "I think I like the 'Til Death Do Us Part' version better."

That is my precious child-bride wife. She loves me unconditionally. She is the best forgiver on the planet. She loves me with a love that, like a bit bull, will not turn me loose no matter what the circumstances. But she is also such a realist and knows that one lifetime together is long enough. Enjoy it while it lasts. Heaven will have other things for us to do.

I tell this story often and people think it is funny, but Janie was not trying to be funny at the time. She was being honest and dead-serious. No pun intended.

Marriage 102

Decades ago, I fell into a romantic mood and bought Janie a small round dining room table for Christmas. I bought it from the Diamond Department store in Charleston, WV. The Diamond was an upscale, multistory shopping venue. It was one of "the places to go" in Charleston. Forget the diamonds and jewelry, guys. Nothing is more romantic than a four-seat dining room table the size of a double large pizza. We still have that little table. The grandkids use it when they come to visit.

"Remember when I bought you that table?" I asked.

"Yes, Christmas 1972, a thousand years ago." She paused. "I didn't want that table. I wanted a bigger one. I still don't like it."

"Then, why do you keep it?"

"Because you bought it for me as a Christmas present- a misguided Christmas present, but a well-intention present, one you put your heart into. So, I keep it because you bought it."

Hey, maybe, it is the thought that counts.

Wuv, Twue Wuv.

Marriage 201

Do not wait for special occasions to express your love. Every day should be a special occasion. Early on during our first year of our marriage, Janie learned to surprise me with little love notes-often accompanied by credit card bills. She had learned to deliver potentially bad news with a message of love as illustrated by the card she gave me one day after a long day of shopping. How could I be upset with someone so loving and thoughtful? (And, yes, we keep everything.)

OUTSIDE   **INSIDE**

Divorce
Circa 2020

Janie has an ongoing feud with our family doctor. He is a nice doctor, and we like him, but he keeps trying to put Janie on new medications. She usually refuses. Although he would not admit it, Janie thinks he gets a little peeved with her, and she has considered changing doctors. However, she does not want to upset him either way.

Before one visit, she predicted that he would recommend a new drug, and she was prepared to tell him no. She had done her research and concluded that that new medication would not be good for her long-term. She was afraid they might have a confrontation.

"Well, how'd it go?" I asked when she came out of the office to get into the car.

"Well, he wanted to put me on that pill I was talking about. I told him no, it wasn't good for me long-term."

"But he's your doctor. He has your best interest in mind."

"Yes, but it's my body, and I know my body."

"Was he upset with you?" I asked further.

"Well, not upset, maybe agitated."

"So, are you and your doctor going to get a divorce?" I asked.

"No, not yet."

"Separated?"

"Oh, not really."

"Thinking of dating someone else?"

"Well, no. Not yet."

"Sleeping in separate beds?"

"Yeah, for the time being."

Janie has been correct about several medications that were at one time recommended by doctors and later pulled from the market because of long-term side effects.

Undying Love

"Tell me you want me to hold you until the stars fall from the sky," I whispered in her ear.
Janie replies, "Are you kidding? I gotta go take my meds."

*****

"Tell me you want me to hold you until the stars fall from the sky," I whispered in her ear.
"I'll have to pee before then."

******

"Tell me you want me to hold you until the stars fall from the sky," I whispered in her ear.
"Oh, wait. Wait. My arm's falling asleep."

*****

"You only say you love me so I will take out the trash," I lamented.
"Well, it doesn't work."

*****

"Tell me you want me to hold you until the stars fall from the sky," I whispered in her ear.
"Wait! Charlie horse! Charlie horse! Oh, oh, oh, Charlie horse!"

The Most Wonderful Person in the World

"Do you really love me?" Janie asked.

"Yes, of course. You are the most wonderful person in the world. Do you love me?"

"Yes, I love you."

"So, why do you get upset with me?" I pondered.

"I said I love you. I didn't say you were the most wonderful person in the world."

The Most Wonderful Person in the World Part 2

"I have changed my mind," Janie announced. "You are the most wonderful person in the world. Have I told you this morning how wonderful you are?"

"Well, no, not yet. Give it a try."

She put her hands on my shoulders and looking intently into my eyes, she said, "You are the most wonderful, sensitive, wise and caring person in the whole world."

"Oh, thank you."

"And I will keep telling you that until it actually comes true."

Hearing Aids, Please

Sometimes I do not hear very well. Janie would say most of the time I do not hear very well.

"What's the name of that actress?" I asked.

"I forget," mumbles Janie.

"Eiffel Get?" I reply.

"Well, at least that's an easy name to remember."

*****

On another occasion, we were at a high school softball game. Our oldest granddaughter was catching. She was a fine little catcher with a great bat and ended her career playing in the state North-South All-Star game. As we were watching the game, a curious announcement came over the loud speaker. I thought it was a promo announcement for the concession stand.

"Cheese sticks, cheese sticks, cheese sticks?" I asked. "Are they selling cheese sticks at the concession stand?"

Janie, leaned over and whispered (loudly) in my ear, "No. Defense, defense, defense."

From that day forward I would yell, "Let's go Cheese Sticks! Let's go Cheese Sticks!"

*****

"I see next year our health care insurance will pay for an annual hearing evaluation," I said.

"Good. I'll go for you."

"What?"

"I'll go for you. I'll just put on the earphones and say, 'Nope, he can't hear that. Nope, he'd never hear that either.'"

*****

"Are you talking to me? Janie asked.
"Sorry. I was talking to myself," I replied.
"You talk louder to yourself than you do to me."
"That's because I'm hard of hearing."

*****

Janie and our daughter, Kim, were in the kitchen. I was at the island working on something important on the laptop, either balancing the checkbook or posting funny memes on Facebook.

"Hey," I called, "can you two quiet down a bit? You are talking so loudly I cannot hear myself think."

"Think louder," came Janie's reply.

Brainy Quotes

In general, here are some of the main differences between men and women. I have learned these through years of passive observation in a domestic setting.

"I want you to do something for me," Janie says. "Go into the classroom (Yes, we have a classroom.) and somewhere in there on a shelf somewhere is a stack, not a bunch, not a pile, a stack of bowls. Metal bowls. Shiny metal bowls. Not plastic bowls. They are really nice bowls that I bought on vacation one year. So, don't drop them. They have something stuffed on top of them. Now, I want you to . . .

"Wait! Hold up," I protested. "My short-term memory buffer is overflowing."

******

"I want you to put this thought in the back of your head," Janie said on another occasion.

"Oh, no," I said in reply. "I can't do that. There's nothing in the back of my head."

******

On another occasion Janie scolded, "You are not listening to me. I told you that before, but you forget everything I say."

"I'm sorry. I can't remember things like you do. My mind is much smaller than yours. It fills up fast."

Way Too Busy

We are eating our typical breakfast at the kitchen island when Janie asks, "What are you going to do today?"
"Nothing," I reply.
"Nothing? But that's what you did yesterday."
"I know. I didn't get finished."

Woozy?

We were on vacation, sitting one morning at a café for breakfast in the New Orleans French Quarter. Unlike the café at the college back in the 60s, the coffee now cost way more than a nickel. I think breakfast cost $80.
Janie rubbed her forehead and remarked, "I getting kind of woozy."
"Perhaps," I offered playfully, "it's because you are in the presence of a very attractive, charming, attentive man."
"Who?" she replied. "The waiter?"

Competition is Serious Business

We were getting ready to play miniature golf. In our family, this is a highly competitive endeavor with big egos at stake.
"I can beat you by twenty strokes," I bragged.
"Well, I can beat you with one," Janie replied, smiling and tapping her putter in the palm of her hand.

Not Just Any Peanut Butter

During the Great Pandemic of 2020, we had been searching high and low for peanut butter cookie dough. We struck out looking in several stores. I finally found some in a Walmart.

"OH, LOOK!" I exclaimed excitedly. "Peanut butter cookie dough!"

Surely, our quest was over. Proudly, I handed the package to Janie. She examined it closely. She was not impressed. I was crushed.

"It's not the kind I have been looking for," she explained.

"But it's PEANUT BUTTER COOKIE DOUGH! We have been looking for this for weeks. We are in the middle of the GREAT PANDEMIC. You cannot find it anywhere else. Sometimes you cannot be choosy," I protested.

She turned the package over in her hand and was silent for what seemed to be an eternity.

"Yeah, I guess it will do, but it wasn't what I expected," she finally said dejectedly.

I thought this was a teachable moment and tried in a gentle, humorous way to show how set in her ways she was. I have thought that on occasions she needs to lower her standards just a bit, especially over something like cookie dough.

"You are so picky sometimes," I observed. "I'm surprised you ever got married." Then I mimicked her voice, "Oh, nice proposal, and you're a really nice guy, and you meet all of my specifications . . . but . . . you're just not what I expected. Go away."

Janie leaned over and whispered in my ear.

"In all honesty, I was getting desperate when you came along."

On another occasion we were shopping for hot chocolate mix. (Caution. Only experienced couples can safely discuss an issue this way.) Nothing I could find would satisfy Janie's specifications. Rejection, again, ran rampant.

Finally, I said, "See, even Walmart in all of its materialistic glory can't satisfy you. I just want you to know how lucky you are to be married to me because sometimes you are so picky and uncompromising and unyielding in what you want that no other man on earth could meet the challenge."

To which she replied, "Picky? Uncompromising? I just know what I want and won't accept anything less."

"But won't you ever lower your standards just a little, especially when your standards can't be met?" I argued.

"Yes, of course. Hey, I chose you, didn't I?"

She is the only person I know who can put you down with a compliment.

The Difference Between Men and Women

We were discussing gifts from Christmas Past. This was like forty-five years Christmas Past.

"Do you remember what I bought you for our first Christmas together?" I asked.

"Yes. A jade bracelet."

"Was it green?"

"Of course, silly. Jade is green. It was green and gold."

"Yeah, I remember that bracelet. Do you remember what you got for me?"

"No."

"Neither do I," I confessed. And then after a moment of contemplation. "You know, Christmas never seems to match my expectations. It's never as romantic or magical as people claim."

"Really?"

"Yes. The reality of Christmas never seems to match the idea of Christmas."

"So, what's your ideal Christmas fantasy?"

"Oh, I don't know," I mused. "Maybe something beyond Hallmark or Norman Rockwell romantic, like just you and me nestled in a quaint mountain cabin, snowed in with three feet of snow, and the pine trees glistening under a full moon. And there we are, just the two of us, snuggled by a roaring fireplace roasting squirrel brains and possum livers."

"Keep dreamin', Henry. We would freeze to death 'cause you can't start a fire, and I don't eat possum livers."

She is such a romantic.

During another Morning Conversation, Janie and I were reading a Facebook post about a couple who relived the 20th anniversary of their first date-in every detail. Well, my first date with Janie was now over fifty years ago, so the details are a little fuzzy.

"Do you remember our first date?" I asked.

"Yes, I do," replied Janie, smiling.

"We went to a football game?"

"That's right. I hate football."

"Then why did you go?"

"I was interested in you, not the football game."
I liked that answer.

"And I didn't have a Harley or a Corvette like Willie, did I?"

Yes, her friend Willie had a Harley motorcycle and a Corvette and took her joy riding all the time before she met me. I never saw her in the Corvette or the back of a bike, but I bet she made them look good. On the other hand, I was driving a broken down 1960 Renault.

"No, you didn't have a bike or fancy car," she confessed.

"So, what did you see in me and not Willie that made you go out with me again?"

"You were taller."

"That's it?" I asked incredulously.

"Yep. That's it. You were taller."

Who says size doesn't matter? She gave up riding Corvettes and Harleys to be with me because I was taller.

Walmart Checkout

While checking out at Walmart during Christmas shopping, I spied a package of Hershey's kisses in our pile of stuff. I picked it up, tossing it about in my hands.

"Do we really need another bag of these? We have like at least a dozen of them at home," I said.

"Yes, I need them. How many times have I told you, don't question me about shopping? I know what I'm doing. I have my reasons."

"But it's my job to question you."

"OK, you're fired."

Janie's Got a Gun

I was waiting in the car for Janie. We were going to go to the gun range to try out a new rifle. She came out of the house, got in the car, and waved a fairly large Bible in the air.

"I wasn't sure if I needed to bring this or not."

I have heard of gun control, but I am speechless on this one. Who brings a Bible to the gun range?

Do not mess with a gun-toting Janie. In the immortal words of Annie Oakley, "I ain't afraid to make love to a man. I ain't afraid to shoot him, either."

I guess the difference between Annie Oakley and Janie is after she shoots you, she will pick up her Bible and pray for you, too.

My Seven Rules for Marriage

Remember, I am not an expert on marriage, but here are my rules for men anyway. I do not have any marriage rules for women. I do not understand women well enough to do that. They are entitled to make up their own rules.

1) It is not a game. Do not keep score.

2) Four eyes see better than two. Sometimes she is smarter than you are.

3) Kiss her early. Kiss her often.

4) If you must fight, choose carefully the hill you wish to die on.

5) Laugh together. Eat together. "Sleep" together. Not necessarily in that order.

6) God can teach you to see her as beautiful today as she was on the first day you fell in love.

7) Carry your own backpack, but let God handle the really tough stuff (heavy burdens).

Rules of the Road
Circa 2019

One of our grandsons, Daven, plays on the high school varsity basketball team. He was just a sophomore but became known as "instant offense," a really good three-point shooter. He comes from good stock. His other grandfather was a state all-star. Daven got his shooting genes from him. I played basketball in high school, too, but usually from the end of the bench. So, my genes give him patience to be content on the bench until it is his time to play.

I also have a relative who played against Jerry West in high school. He will proudly boast that he held Jerry to forty points one night. So, I guess Daven inherited his braggadocio from my relative.

But I digress.

We were running late for a ballgame and went to a drive-thru to grab something quick to eat. As we pulled out, Janie made her announcement.

"We are not eating in the car in the dark."

"What?"

"We are not eating in the car in the dark."

"But the food will get cold."

"We are not eating in the car in the dark while you are driving."

I was surprised. No eating in the car?

"That's a new rule," I said. "I have never heard of that rule before."

"Yes, a new rule for an old driver."

"We have been driving at night for years, and I am sure we have eaten in the dark at seventy miles per hour."

"You don't drive so well anymore. Your reflexes aren't so good."

"I still have good reflexes."

"Look out for that deer!"

42

I hit the brakes, desperately looking for a deer.

"I don't see a deer."

"See," said Janie, "your eyesight is going, too."

Wow, I thought, by the time we get to the game she will have me in an old folks' home.

"Hey, wait. There was no deer, was there?" I challenged.

Even in the dark, speeding along with my eyes fixed on the road looking for invisible critters, I could see she was smiling.

"No, there was no deer. But you still cannot eat and drive."

"You could hand it to me, bite by bite."

"I could stuff it in your mouth," she said slowly.

Do not worry folks. I know my wife. She does not really mean it, and she knows I know she knows she does not really mean it. She is just saying this for emphasis. She is telling me to wrap up this conversation; I am not going to win. So, relax folks. I know how to handle this.

I appealed to her romantic side, pointing out my worthiness as a mate. Seriously, she does have a romantic side. You just need to know how to approach it—never through the front door. You have to slip in carefully through a side window.

"You do know there is only one person in this whole world who could live with you and all of your silly rules and still give you four kids and eleven grandkids."

She chuckled.

"You know, you're right. I am fortunate to have someone who puts up with me . . . but you're still not eating in the car in the dark."

So, I looked forward to eating my cold sandwich in the school parking lot.

43

It's Five O'clock Somewhere

"Why do you set the alarm for 5:30am every day?" I asked.

"Because I can get up in time to get Kim off to work."

"But she doesn't work every day."

"I know, but I also know the alarm works. I don't have to worry about forgetting to set it. It doesn't wake me up. I just turn it off and go back to sleep on the days Kim does not work."

"But it's not all about you," I protested. "It wakes the dog up too, and she thinks it's time to go out and bark at the lawn, and I have to get out of bed and let her out and then get back up and let her in. And then I find myself wide awake with nothing to do but watch you sleep."

"I bet that's entertaining."

A Tip About Dreaming

I woke up screaming in the middle of the night.

"What's wrong.? Are you OK?"

"I was having a nightmare. I was dreaming someone was in the room with us, but I couldn't see them because it was dark. Whatever it was kept moving around the room, but I could not see it because I could not find the light switch."

"See," Janie told me, "I have told you before, you should always dream with the lights on."

In a strange, metaphorical sense, I think she is right.

Dream. Dream big, but always keep yourself rooted in reality. Don't allow you dreams to cloud your vision of reality. To quote Shakespeare, "I grant I never saw a goddess go; My mistress, when she walks, treads on the ground."

Passionate Kisses

With our 45th anniversary coming up, Janie and I were talking about when we were dating and how we fell in love. I offered my version.

"Remember when we drove up to Hawks Nest in the mountains and looked out over the gorge-and held each other in our arms and kissed?"

"Yes."

"And in that moment, we knew we were meant for each other?"

"Well, that's not when it happened. Do you know when I knew?"

"When?"

"The first time you kissed me goodnight at my door."

"Really?"

"Yes. You kissed me and I knew we fit. We just fit."

"Really? Seriously?"

"Yes, we just-fit."

She had a rare, dreamy, far-away look in her eyes, and I realized she was being serious. This was perhaps the most genuinely romantic moment of her entire love-career. I could tell by her body language that she was moved by the memory. So, she knew on the first date, after the first kiss? What a revelation.

"You are kidding me. The very first kiss?" I said in disbelief.

"Yes. Actually, halfway through the very first kiss, I knew you were the one."

"So," I said, "you're saying I wasted my gas driving to Hawks Nest?"

The Importance of Simon and Garfunkel
(A Real-Life Parable)

I shall never forget the day when I discovered Janie did not like Simon and Garfunkel. I was highly disappointed and depressed. If I had known of her lack of passion for Paul Simon music before we were married that might have been a game-changer. But we were married; had been for years. We had four children, for goodness sakes, and now I discover this dark, hidden secret about her? What was I to do now?

At first, I was in denial. How could someone so sweet and beautiful not like Paul Simon? (Hey, who really cares about Garfunkel?) How could she have such a huge character flaw? And then I started blaming myself. Where did I go wrong in the dating process that this vital piece of information was not uncovered? And then I started doubting her. What other horrible, dark secrets was she hiding from me-for years? What would I learn next?

Then I began to ask: does she have some redeeming quality that would compensate or offset this hole in our relationship? Sadly, the answer was no. After much soul searching and introspection, I resigned myself to a marriage without a Paul-Simon-music-loving partner. And you know what? Over time Paul became less and less important in my life. In time, I learned to appreciate her style of music-serious, sophisticated artists like Tony Orland and Dawn, and Tom Jones. Yeah-Tie a yellow ribbon 'round the old oak tree, Pussycat.

And so, from the depths of my heart I forgave her for not liking *Still Crazy After All These Years, the Sounds of Silence, The Boxer, and Rene and Georgette Magritte* with their dog after the war.

Eventually, God blessed me for my magnanimity through my oldest son. As he grew into a teenager, miraculously he developed a taste for Paul Simon music. As we would drive down the road, he who would reach into the glove compartment and get our hidden Graceland CD- but only if Janie was not with us. I loved her enough to not subject her to *The Boy in the Bubble*. After all, a constellation was dying in the corner of the sky. She would not like a song like that, but Son John did and who am I to blow against the wind?

Oh, the sacrifices made for love. I got *Diamonds on the Soul of My Shoes*.

Advanced Marriage 501

Remember, again, I am not an expert on marriage, but as an old codger, I am going to give you some basic life-skills advice, so listen up. It is free. It may also be worthless. I will let you decide.

I have a picture of Janie on my smartphone. I see that picture every time I look at my phone. This is a constant reminder of the beauty of Janie's smile and a reflection of the true beauty that is in her heart and soul. Now, I do not believe that you can create your own reality simply through positive thinking, but I do know this: keeping this mental picture of her strength, love, and beauty crowds out and overpowers any negative thing that may come along in our relationship.

The picture is also a reminder of the time when we took silly birthday pictures at Kroger and the fun we had while doing that simple little excursion. We went through the store, and Janie picked out items for her birthday gifts-flowers, candy, cards, etc. We would take a picture with her holding her "gift" and then put it back on the shelf. Remember, I am cheap. She got to hold several presents that day, at least for a minute or two.

I cannot look at that picture on my phone without smiling and feeling blessed. Yes, we have had our spats, and our disagreements, and our verbal battles, and our childish temper tantrums. No, we are not perfect. We do not pretend to be. But one thing we have NEVER done is take pictures of the bad things, the low times, the trying experiences.

If you looked through our photos, all you will find are happy times, fun times, important times, times of significance and meaning, times of celebration. For us, there are no photos of the "Big Blow up of '77" or the "Great Health Crisis of 2001" or the "Great Swimming Pool Custody Battle of 2014" that we can pull out and "admire" and talk about and rekindle all of those negative emotions. Ain't gonna, happen, folks.

In the same way, with God's help, each of us can train our minds to filter out the bad stuff—to cast it into the sea of forgetfulness, so to speak and keep only the good stuff in our memory banks. This is not a naive denial of the bad things that happen from time to time. Rather it is a resolve that those bad things are transient, temporary, and in the long run not worthy to be remembered. You cannot change yesterday, but you can start today to change the future by first cleaning out your memory banks and then start filling them with only good stuff.

And speaking of challenges, the next story is about one that has lasted decades.

Kim's Story

Early on Easter Sunday in the early 80s, Janie was in labor with our fourth child, Kim. We rushed to the hospital, and she quickly delivered. After four kids, she did not believe in long labors. I then rushed back to church to narrate the Easter cantata. It was a joyous but uneventful birth. Only men can claim a birth was uneventful. We were now ready to cruise on down the road of life as a happy, normal family of six. However, over the next few months we learned that Kim was severely hearing impaired. Over the next few years, we learned she had other disabilities as well.

Let me tell you, having a hearing-impaired child, having a child with disabilities was a shock. It was the last thing on our radar screen of life. It was something truly unexpected that God brought into our lives. But as journalist Tony Snow once said, "God relishes surprise. We want lives of simple, predictable ease-smooth, even trails as far as the eye can see, but God likes to go off-road. He provokes us with twists and turns. He places us in predicaments that seem to defy our endurance; and comprehension-and yet don't. By His love and grace, we persevere. The challenges that make our hearts leap and stomachs churn invariably strengthen our faith and grant measures of wisdom and joy we would not experience otherwise."

And so, God took us "off-road" with Kim.

Almost continuous illnesses and other medical problems prevented her from acquiring language during those critical developmental years. When she started in school, her speech was mostly unintelligible. She could barely speak in three-word sentences. Although she had some excellent individual teachers, she never could catch up and, in fact, fell further and further behind.

During second grade, she gave up completely. She gave up learning, progressing, even trying. As the year progressed, she withdrew more and more into her little cocoon. She could not tell you the answers to some of the most basic questions: "What day of the week is it?", "How much is two plus two?" With glazed-over eyes, her standard reply to almost every question was "I don't know."

In second grade, the teacher abandoned her. Kim was given a coloring book. She would sit in the back of the room and scribble while the teacher worked with the other students. After a battery of tests, she was judged to be "multi-handicapped" and was going to be treated that way by the school system. They told us she would never learn how to speak or read or write at a functional level. We refused to accept that answer.

We knew at that point only two people in the world could rescue Kim-me and Janie. However, we had no idea what do to. We began to search for alternatives. Listen up; this is important. You do not have to have things all figured out ahead of time when God is leading. You just have to take the next step. And so, before we started our search, we prayed that God would open doors and close doors and lead us to the right thing to do for Kim. We looked at Christian schools, private schools, public schools in other counties, the schools for the deaf, etc. All along the way God was faithful. He closed doors and he opened doors until we knew the right path-home schooling.

I turned a bedroom into a classroom and taught Kim math. Janie literally sacrificed her life for the next twelve to fifteen years to work with Kim on a daily basis. I think you know my wife well enough by now to know it was a willing sacrifice of love-a pit bull type of love. The journey was not easy, but all along the way God was leading. He brought teachers, parents, school administrators, specialists and knowledgeable people into our lives that supported us in everything we did. Over time, we had a support system for obtaining new ideas, approaches, resources, and teaching techniques. God gave us hope in the valleys and joy on the mountains and strength in times or trials.

Slowly, Kim proved the experts wrong. She learned to read and write and carry on a conversation. She will proudly tell you that she used to work at Toys R Us until it went out of business. She folds bulletins at church and on occasion does work at her sister's law office.

The journey, however, is never ending. The struggle for normalcy is still a daily one, but with God's help we all will continue to persevere. This little poem I wrote sums up our daily struggle.

> Sometimes in anger I've asked You,
> But often with most bitter tear,
> If You made the earth and the heavens
> Then why can my daughter not hear?
>
> I don't want her labeled as "special"
> An excuse to push her aside.
> I want folks to look past her frailty
> To see the blossoming beauty inside.
>
> But I've seen as she labors in learning,
> And heard as she struggles to speak,
> And she's taught me with each hard-fought victory
> 'Tis I, and not she, who is weak.
>
> For she's overcome much more in ten years
> Than I have in my forty or so,
> And she's taught me a life-long lesson:
> Sometimes the victories come slow.

So, we'll persevere till we've vanquished
Every fear, every failure and foe,
And be better off for the battle
In which she, and I also, will grow.

Lord, thank you for sending her to us
Made in her own unique way.
I'm certain there is a day coming
When I, and she also, will say:

I've played my life's hand to the fullest.
And overcome much more than most.
For my spunk and indomitable spirit
Not in I, but in you, Lord, will boast.

Send the Very Best and Other Stuff

"Hallmark called. My Christmas ornament is ready for pickup," Janie informed me.

She hurried out the door to go pick it up. Getting her annual Hallmark Christmas ornament was one of the highlights of her Christmas season. When she returned with her "prize," I looked at the receipt. I was shocked.

"This ornament cost $36?" I queried. "I thought these special Christmas ornaments were free-like a frequent shopper reward."

"No silly, they are not free. Hallmark was just holding it for me."

"Holding it?" I replied incredulously. "Holding it for what? Ransom?"

******

"I've been looking all day for some real cute tops, but I can't find any," Janie lamented.

"Have you tried looking in your closet?"

Welcome to the danger zone.

******

"I'm sorry if I hurt your feelings. I didn't mean to. If I had, I would have done better," Janie said.

"Done better at what? Hurting my feelings?"

"Oh, yes. If I really wanted to hurt your feelings, I know I would have done a much better job."

Inconvenient Cooking Truth

Sometimes, Janie can humble me with a few little words.

She was recuperating from back surgery, and most of the household chores fell to me. I was already doing some of those domestic maintenance tasks. Two years earlier, I bought her a really nice vacuum cleaner for Christmas. Yes, a traditional yuletide gift of love. A vacuum cleaner. However, she has never used it because I do all the vacuuming. If she tells me that she loves me, I try to take out the trash, and I do help with the laundry, but I have left most of the cooking to her. I can nuke something in the microwave or fix a peanut butter and jelly sandwich, but I am lost beyond that.

However, with Janie on the mend, I needed to step up. So, I volunteered to fix dinner. I had cleaned out the freezer and found some frozen mastodon stuffed peppers dated from 1492 in the bottom. I planned to pop that into the oven, open a can of corn and pull some leftover slaw out of the frig-a simple but adequate meal, I thought.

Before long, however, Janie was giving me instructions on making roasted potatoes with a very detailed, step-by-step process for washing, cutting up the potatoes, applying spices, turning them, etc. After that, she was instructing me on how to prepare wilted lettuce.

I looked at her and smiled.

"I was planning on baking some of your fossilized mastodon meat, opening a can of corn, pouring it in a pot and turning on the heat. This looks like a lot more work to me."

"Yes, it is," she replied. "So, what's your problem?"

"Hey, I volunteered to fix dinner," I reminded her.

"Well, so do I," she replied. "Every day."

Bazinga!!

Music to Cook By

Janie was instructing me on how to cook spaghetti, part of my on-the-job emergency culinary training.

"You need to put a little olive oil in the noodles to keep them from sticking together," she said.

"How much is a little?" I asked.

"Just take the bottle and pour it like 'eeenk'," she explained, motioning quickly with her hand.

That was an odd way of measuring ingredients, I thought. I had heard of a teaspoon or even a pinch or a dash, but never an audible "eeenk."

"An eeenk?" I asked for clarification. "How much is that?"

"Just tip the bottle over and say eeenk and then stop pouring. That should be the right amount."

"Eeenk, huh? OK. Is that a C sharp eeenk?"

"No, dummy, D flat."

Never try to outsmart someone who knows her music.

One Dreaded Christmas Eve
(Circa late 1980s)

I used to dread Christmas Eve when the kids were young. Now do not get me wrong. I like Christmas. I like the decorations. I enjoy the plays and cantatas. I love the food and festivities. I even like fruitcake. However, basically two things about Christmas used to bother me. One I simply disliked. The other I dreaded with mortal fear.

What I used to dislike was our annual shopping trip to the mall. Believe it or not, we once lived in an area that was so far from civilization that the nearest mall was eighty miles away. Janie always insisted on loading up the little kids (I think we had three of them at the time.) for a day of shopping at the mall. She said we were making memories, building a family Christmas tradition. I always thought she watched too many "Father Knows Best" episodes when she was young.

For the life of me, I never understood how a day-long-kid-laden-torture-trip to the mall could possibly build happy family memories. This "tradition" came nowhere close to roasting chestnuts by an open fire or walking in a winter wonderland. To me it was more like a Spanish Inquisition torture chamber. It took two hours to get there, the prices were always higher than anywhere else, and by ten o'clock I was worn out and ready for a long winter's nap. By noon the kids were exhausted and cranky. They had no desire to shop, no desire to eat, and no desire to see Santa Claus. The "30% Off" sale signs meant nothing to either me or them. All we wanted to do was go home. But all in all, the annual mall trip was bearable, if not pleasant, and I must admit it did generate a lot of yuletide memories.

What I really dreaded was Christmas Eve. When the

kids were young, the ritual was usually the same. We would load them up in the car for a trip through the neighborhood to see the lights and decorations. Then we would return home and settle in for the night where we would have a little family devotion about the Christ Child from the gospel of Luke. After that we would open one present and leave the rest for morning. The children would then reluctantly go to bed early, and Janie and I would have the rest of the evening to ourselves.

What is to dread, you ask? With the kids tucked safely in bed, would this not be an excellent opportunity to share a cup of coffee and some fruitcake with your spouse? Perhaps you could meditate on the joys and wonders of Christmas. Perhaps it would be a good time to reflect back on the happy times of the past year. Or maybe you could put on some soft Christmas music, turn out the lights, and watch the Christmas tree sparkle and glow. Perhaps you could even slide into a little romantic interlude. (Yes, even after three kids, a romantic interlude is totally appropriate.) But, oh no, it never happened that way. At least, at our house it never happened that way.

As soon as the kids were tucked away-as quickly as you could hum "God rest ye merry gentlemen"-Panic Time arrived. It was also known as "Mission Impossible." With the kids in bed, it was time to haul out the presents from Santa and put them under the tree. Invariably, one of the kid's most wanted toys was hidden away in a closet somewhere. As loving child-bride wife Janie would haul it into the living room, I would spot on the side of the box one of the most dreaded phrases known to mankind-at least one of the most dreaded phrases known to fatherhood- "Some Assembly Required."

Here is how it went one dreaded Christmas Eve at our house.

"Do we have to put that thing together tonight?" I

protested. "Can't we just relax here by the fireplace?"

"Not until we've put this together," came Janie's firm reply.

"But -"

"No 'buts.' Little John-John expects this to be under the tree in the morning-totally assembled and working."

"But -"

"I told him Santa was going to bring it, and Santa would never leave a toy unassembled."

"You shouldn't have told him that. He doesn't believe in Santa Claus."

"I know that, and you know that-and he knows that, but he still likes to play the game. He thinks he gets more presents that way."

"Well, does he? Get more presents by believing in Santa Claus, I mean."

"Don't ask. You don't want to know."

She was right. I did not want to know.

I looked at the box. It did not look very big or complicated. Last year she had bought a detailed replica of the entire Star Wars battle fleet. There were twelve million little parts to it, and I had to piece them all together one by one before I could go to bed. But did she care? Not in your life. Her only concern was that little John-John would not be disappointed in the morning.

"Let me see that," I said reluctantly. "That doesn't look too bad. What is it?"

"It's a two-story automobile service center for his matchbox cars."

A two-story automobile service center? Who had ever heard of a two-story auto repair shop?

"Can't this wait 'til morning?" I asked desperately.

"No. He's been asking for this since Labor Day-Fourth of July, actually, and I don't want him to wait one more day."

I heaved a sigh of resignation and opened the box. I looked at the instructions for a minute and then, in disgust, I threw them into the fireplace.

"Why did you do that?" my loving child-bride wife gasped.

"Because those instructions were worthless. They were written in French."

"There was English on the backside, Hon."

"Oh," I said. "Wish you'd have told me that sooner."

The world had only recently started printing instructions in multiple languages, and I was still struggling with this culture change.

No instructions. I burned up the instruction. Oh, well, how difficult could it be? I took a look at the picture on the box. On the bottom level was a garage door that led to an elevator. The elevator was used to lift the car to the second-floor service area. And leading down from the second level was a ramp that would shoot your car across the floor. Piece of cake, I thought. I would have this thing put together in no time flat. That should leave me plenty of time for coffee sipping, fruitcake nibbling, Christmas meditation, and perhaps a little cuddling. I proceeded to dump the parts out on the floor.

"This thing is made of cardboard!" I exclaimed in surprise.

"So?" my loving child-bride wife responded.

"Well, I work for a chemical company. We make plastic. Plastic is the wave of the future. You should always buy plastic. It lasts longer."

"But this is exactly what little John-John wanted," she said defensively.

Cardboard. What a piece of junk, I thought. But I did not dare say that out loud.

"How much did you pay for this?"

"Don't ask," she said defensively. "You don't want to

know."

She was right. I did not want to know.

OK, I thought, I will buckle down and get this thing put together and little John-John will be happy. After all, what else did I have to do on Christmas Eve?

To my surprise after about a half hour, I had all the cardboard tabs safely secured into all the little cardboard slots, and all the tiny decals were plastered in all the right spots. I stood back and admired my handiwork. Not bad, I thought, not bad at all. It looked just like the station that was pictured on the box.

"Looks pretty nice, doesn't it?" I said, quite proud of my accomplishment.

"Yep, pretty good. And you thought it would be a lot of trouble to put together."

"Well, I guess sometimes you get lucky," I said.

"And now for the test," my loving child-bride wife proclaimed.

"Test? What test? What are you gonna test?"

She approached the station with something in her hand.

"Don't touch that thing," I warned. "It's all right right where it is."

Janie ignored my warnings. Taking a little matchbox car, she placed it in the elevator and turned the crank. To my amazement, it worked. The elevator actually worked. Thank goodness it worked. She then pushed the car around in the service bay and positioned it at the top of the ramp.

"Bombs away!" she said, giving the car a push with her index finger.

The little car shot down the ramp and raced across the floor. Janie sat back and beamed with satisfaction.

"Little John-John will be so pleased," she said as she came closer to give me a hug. "And I'm so proud of you, Honey. You handled that like a real m-"

Suddenly something caught the corner of her eye that stopped her in mid-sentence. Instinctively, I turned to look at the garage. My heart sank. It had collapsed into complete shambles.

"Oh, no," I said, covering my eyes with my hand.

"Oh, you can fix it," she encouraged me. "It probably just needs a little adjustment."

Well, two hours later, I was still adjusting, but no matter what I did for some mysterious reason the garage would collapse every time a car went racing down the ramp. Finally, my patience had run out. After considerable effort, I managed to piece that abomination together one last time. In disgust, I placed it under the tree.

"There. Don't you dare touch it," I warned. And finally, I verbalized what I had been thinking all along. "That cardboard abomination is a piece of junk!"

As soon as I had said that, I knew I was in trouble. Big trouble. Big Christmas Eve trouble. My loving child-bride wife puckered up, her eyes got misty, and her voice cracked with emotion.

"You don't know what I went through to find that thing," she cried. "And you don't know how much little John-John really wants that garage. And now you've gone and ruined it all! You've ruined the garage. You've ruined Christmas!"

Me? I've ruined it all? I've ruined Christmas? Not me. It was that abominable cardboard garage that ruined Christmas. It was "Some Assembly Required" that ruined Christmas. I had gone above and beyond the call of duty. I should have been getting combat pay. And I hate it when she cries-especially when there is nothing that I can do about it.

"Look, leave that thing right there under the tree and don't touch it. Maybe John-John will know how to fix it in the morning," I suggested.

"But-"

"I've had it, Jane. I'm going to bed, and no, I don't want any coffee and fruitcake, and no, I don't want to sit and reflect on the joys of Christmas, or watch the logs burn in the fireplace, or any of those other things that loving couples are supposed to do on Christmas Eve. Just get me away from that piece of junk before I throw it in the fire!"

That night I had a hard time going to sleep on our couch. Yes, my loving child-bride wife had relegated me to the couch.

That night every time I turned over I got a glimpse of that infernal garage sitting under the tree. I was afraid to really look at it for very long because I was afraid just looking at it would make it collapse. I had visions of the entire Christmas tree collapsing, and heaven help me if it did. Janie would never believe that I had not touched it.

Early the next morning, Christmas morning, a sleepy-eyed daughter poked her head into the room. Her mother, my loving child-bride wife, was close behind her.

"Mom, why is Daddy sleeping in here?"

"Oh, he's guarding the presents, dear." She gave me a smirk. "Last night a mean old grinch was here trying to throw all of them into the fire."

I smiled a fake smile as I propped myself up on one elbow.

Just then little John-John came running into the room and looked around excitedly. There was only one thing on his little six-year-old mind.

"My auto garage!" he exclaimed. "Oh, thank you, Mom. Thank you, thank you, thank you."

"Santa brought it last night," she said.

"Right, Mom, right," little John-John replied, sounding so grown up. "You know I don't believe in Santa anymore."

"Ssssh," I said. "Your little brother still believes in

Santa Claus, so you've still got to play along for another year. OK?"

"OK," agreed John-John in a whisper. His face was beaming as he picked up his beloved garage and raced off toward his bedroom. He did not even look at his other gifts.

A little later Janie and I were sitting at the kitchen table belatedly sipping coffee and munching on fruitcake. Apologies were exchanged. We hugged and kissed and made up. All was right with the world again.

Just then little John-John came in and plopped his now broken-down garage on the table. It had fallen apart again.

"It's broken," he said with a forlorn frown on his face.

"Oh, honey," said Janie, "I'm so sorry. But don't worry. Daddy will fix it."

"Mom," said little John-John pensively, "I think I still believe in Santa Claus."

"You do?"

"Yep. I think he must be real."

"You do, honey? Why?"

"Because you and Dad would never buy me a piece of junk like this."

Kiss an Angel Good Morning, Not

Janie opened her eyes, turned my way, and mumbled hello.

"I've been awake since 4:00 o'clock," I informed her.

"Really?" she said, wiping the sleep from her eyes.

"Yeah. I was watching you sleep. For two whole hours you didn't move at all. No twisting or turning. No sound. No snoring. Not a single detectable movement. You were absolutely motionless for two hours."

"And you watched me sleep? For two hours? That's so sweet."

"Not really," I replied. "I thought you might be dead, but I knew if I checked and you weren't dead, I would wake you up, and then I would be in big trouble for doing that because last night you said, 'Don't wake me up in the morning.' So, I just watched. It was kind of fascinating, and I figured if you were really dead, I didn't want to know anyway."

"Good choice," she said as she rolled away from me, closed her eyes and went back to sleep.

A Random Thought About Marriage

Stand back about four feet at an angle to a window. Close your right eye. Look out. Now close the left eye, open the right and look out. You will notice two different views of what is outside the window. Some objects around the edge of your vision will disappear in one eye and be visible in the other.

Now open both eyes and you get a composite view. Your brain does that little trick for you. It puts the two images together for you. You only have one mind, and it sees only one picture even though your eyes actually see different things.

In the same way, that is the way marriage should be: two people, each with one eye so to speak, seeing with different perspectives but united and blended together with one mind into a common view of the world. The end result is a more encompassing, composite view that is not possible with only one person.

In other words, marriage consists of two half-blind people who are helping each other stumble down the road of life. The trick is being open to allowing your partner to tell you about things you may not be able to see.

It also helps tremendously if both of you are looking through the same window.

Going to the Dogs
(Circa early 1990s)

"If those stupid dogs come into *my* house, I'm leaving!"

I was desperate.

I was losing the battle.

I was quickly running out of options.

It was now the 1990s, and we had four children. Four stubborn and independently-minded kids. They were all clones of their mother's disposition. And they were all conspiring against me, the supposed head of the house.

I had tried reason. "They're expensive." "They'll soil the carpet." "They'll cost a fortune in vet bills." "They'll shed all over the couch." "They'll kill the cats." Reason did not work.

I had tried diplomacy. "I know you all want a dog, but shouldn't you respect my opinions, too?" Diplomacy did not work.

I tried bribery. "The money we'd save on dog food can be used to go to Disney World." "If you want your allowances, kids, you'll agree with me." Bribery failed miserably.

I tried to throw my weight around. "I'm the head of this house, and I say NO DOGS." No one paid any attention.

And so, I was down to my last negotiating ploy-call it an appeal for sympathy. "Choose ye this day whom ye shall love-me or the dogs."

I was serious. If those dogs moved in, I was moving out. The rest of the family would have to make a serious decision. Either they would continue to have my company (and income) or they could have a couple of flea-bitten dogs sleeping on the sofa and pooping in the hallway.

Surely, that would stop those two mutts from becoming part of the family. Daughter Maggie was in college and one of her professors gave her two so-called dogs. They were supposedly purebred, pedigreed. That did not impress me.

"I'm dead serious about this. It's me or the dogs," I challenged.

But early the next morning, despite my pleas, protests, and tantrums, the front door opened and my oldest daughter deposited two brown and black dust rags inside the front door. Much to my amazement the two dust rags started yapping and raced up the stairs.

"Those are dogs?" I asked. "Where are their eyes?"

Maggie scooped one up and brushed the hair from its eyes.

"Right here," she said.

"And you call this thing a dog?" I asked again.

"This is Josephine Morgan, the Crazy Circus Dog," Maggie said proudly. "She's a Yorkshire Terrier and she weights three and a half pounds!"

"Is that before or after we cook her for dinner?" I asked sarcastically.

"Dad! Don't be so cruel."

"Look. I told you it was me or them. Don't expect me to like them."

"But Dad, this is Josephine Morgan, the Crazy Circus Dog."

"The Crazy Circus Dog?"

"Yea."

Maggie held Josey, short for Josephine, in one hand above her head. She proceeded to tell a story about Josephine Morgan, the Crazy Circus Dog, who wandered around the Big Top talking to all the other animals. As she told her goofy story, she was flopping Josephine Morgan around like a puppet. Occasionally, she would put Josey down and the little dog would immediately spin around two or three times and leap back into my daughter's arms. The story was so off-the-wall and little Josey, with all of her shaggy-haired energy, was so silly looking that I had to suppress a smile. Inside I chuckled, but outside I was grim-faced. After all, I was about to abandon my family, I was poised on the brink of homelessness over two dogs. I could not let them know that Josey was cute.

"And the other one?" I asked. "What's her name?"

"Tessa Marie. She weighs 5 pounds."

"A real porker, eh? Got a stupid nickname like the other one?" I was trying to muster all the grouchiness that I could.

"Nope, just Tessa Marie. She thinks she's a grizzly bear."

Janie was cradling Tessa in her forearm. Tessa looked at me. At least I think she looked at me. Sometimes it is hard to tell which end is which with all that hair. Anyway, she looked at me and smiled! There among all the hair was the neatest little row of white teeth. My defeat was complete.

"OK. All right. They can stay."

Just then my son came down the hallway lugging something heavy.

"Here's your suitcase, Dad. I heard you were leaving."

Defeat was not enough. They had to humiliate me to boot.

"Take that thing back to the bedroom," I commanded.

"But we thought you were leaving," Janie said with a smile.

"I am," I said, trying to save face. "I'm just not ready to go yet."

Almost two years have passed since I said that. I wonder if they have forgotten my threat?

It would not be long before Tessa had a sleeping spot in Janie's bed. Technically, it is my bed, too, but I would never admit to having a dust-rag dog that thinks she is a grizzly bear sleeping in *my* bed.

I came up with the perfect nickname for Tessa. First, she got into the Halloween candy and ate a bunch of peppermint patties-aluminum foil and all. We had to rush her to the veterinarian to get her stomach pumped. Chocolate can kill a dog, and the aluminum could stop up her digestive tract. On another occasion, she needed surgery to get the aluminum out of her digestive tract. I had warned the whole family that dogs are expensive, but they did not care. They were using my money.

Not long after that, my son had to make plastic for a science project. He had to make it using of some kind of egg, milk, and starch formula. On Saturday night, Joey cooked up his first batch of plastic and left it on the kitchen table to dry. We do not know how, but Tessa, who only stands about eight inches high, managed to get up on the table and devour Joey's project. On Sunday morning, Joey was frantic because it took two days for the plastic to dry out. However, we were able to calm him down. He cooked up another batch. This time we placed it on the table in front of a fan for drying and took extra precautions to keep Tessa off the table.

On Monday morning only minutes before leaving for school, Joey carefully sealed his plastic-egg project in a plastic margarine container. That is when he made his fateful mistake. He sat the container on top of his book bag which was in the floor. Within seconds, a loud scream of "Oh, no!" came from the living room. Tessa had torn open the container and Joey and his mom were chasing her under the dining room table. Too late. We could not believe it, but she had eaten the whole thing-again-all within a matter of seconds.

When Joey told his teacher that his dog had eaten his project, not once, but twice, she believed him. No one had ever given her that excuse before. She figured it had to be true.

Well, after that, and after Tessa ballooned from five to ten pounds, I concluded that she had gained the right to be called Miss Piggy. Janie says that it is not nice to talk to the poor dog that way. But when I say it real lovingly and scratch her under the chin, Tessa does not seem to mind at all. After all, the little porker does not speak English.

More Random Conversations

"Hey, look! Here's a guy on TV advertising a book called *Have a Better Sex Life by Saturday*," I said.

Janie, dryly, laconically, "Which Saturday?"

******

"Where's the Advil?" I called to Janie in the next room.

"In the cupboard next to the frig."

"How many do I take?"

"Adults take two."

"So, I take two?"

Silence.

******

The morning of New Year's Day rolled around. As we were enjoying breakfast, I leaned over from my coffee and kissed Janie.

"This year we are going to be the perfect couple," I told my loving child-bride wife.

"You mean I wasn't the perfect mate last year?"

******

"You don't like my new book, do you?" I lamented. The book I was talking about sits somewhere in the corner of my hard drive, unpublished. Someday, when I am long gone, it will probably get published, a movie made from it, I will be incredibly famous, and Janie will be incredibly wealthy. The book is called *Conversations with a Stranger* and is marginally a science fiction book. I like it a lot, but seriously, I have never tried to publish it.

"I didn't say I didn't like it. I said I like it, but I like your other books better. This one is just not my style."

For the record, the book also falls into the hillbilly-nostalgic-pseudo-history-sci-fi--human-interest genre, a very small niche with an audience of about 142 people or so.

"But you're supposed to like it," I protested. "You're supposed to say it's the greatest literary work in the last five hundred years."

"Do you want the truth? Do you want my honest opinion or do you want me to lie?"

"To be honest, I want you to lie."

*****

"Look, Tudor's drive-thru is backed-up into the street," I observed.

"We've had this conversation before."

"I know."

"Can we have another, more meaningful conversation?"

"Not as long as Tudor's is backed-up."

******

"You know, I don't know anything about the Korean War," Janie confessed.

"It was a war in Korea. We shot at the Koreans. They shot at us," I explained.

"Which Koreans?"

"We shot at the North Koreans. The Chinese-backed Communist Koreans."

"See. I didn't know that. We never studied that in history class."

"That's because when you were in school it wasn't history. It was current events."

******

73

"Are we gonna take a little drive through the mountains and look at the fall foliage?" I asked.

"No. Too busy. Don't have time."

"Maybe," I suggested, "we can schedule something after you pass away."

"Yep, that'll work."

******

"What is that goo?" Janie asks.

"I don't know, but I saw it in a movie once. After about fifteen minutes everyone was screaming, fleeing in panic. It did not end well."

******

Jane, patting my knee, "Hey, you awake?"

"What," I respond groggily as I awaken from sleep.

"Oh, good. You're awake. Are you going with us to Kim's doctor's appointment on Monday?"

"You woke me up on a Friday night to ask about an appointment on Monday?"

"You fall asleep too fast."

******

"I need a body transplant," I lamented over my aches and pains.

"Really?"

"Yeah. I just can't wait until they can download your brain and then upload it into a brand-new body."

"For you, that wouldn't fix anything."

The Infamous Class Reunion Caper

Janie's 50th high school class reunion came much too soon, but remember, she is an older woman by fifteen months. We live a short distance from her school, so we go to her reunions almost every year. Usually, they are boring, uneventful affairs. Since I did not go to her high school, I knew very few people at these reunions. Four to be exact, not counting Janie. There was Mary and Terry and Joyce and Rick. We use to go to church with Terry and Mary, and Janie was Joyce's bridesmaid. Oh, yeah, and Willie, Janie's motorcycle and Corvette riding partner. I forgot Willie would be there, too. Willie is a really sweet guy who accepted my rise to prominence with Janie. He lived near the high school, and we would go visit with him from time to time. However, I do not remember him ever offering me a ride in his Corvette.

This year was going to be different. Before the reunion, Janie received a call from another old boyfriend. A serious old boyfriend. He was coming to the reunion for the first time since the Battle of 1812. I was not sure how I felt about this. Old boyfriend. 50th reunion. Nostalgia. They had not seen each other in decades. There was going to be lots of talk about the good old days. Well, you never know where that would lead.

When we got to the reunion, Janie stopped at the registration desk, and I went on inside the ballroom. I spotted her old boyfriend immediately. I had never seen him before, but I recognized who he was right off. He was standing at the table with Rick and Joyce. He looked like someone Janie would be attracted to. Of course, he was not nearly as handsome as I was. Advantage me. I began sizing up the competition. We were about the same height and weight. OK, toss up. He looked a lot older than me. I actually look twenty years younger than I am. Good, I thought. Janie likes younger men. Advantage me. He had a goatee. Janie dislikes facial hair. Advantage me. Hmmmm. Maybe I'll be OK after all.

I was bold and slightly confident, so I went over to old-boyfriend and introduced myself. He smiled and shook my hand. He was probably thinking, "So, you're the one who stole my girlfriend?"

"Where's Janie?" he asked.

I motioned toward the door.

"Over by the registration desk."

He looked over and saw her.

"Ah, yes. I would recognize her anywhere."

She looked over and saw him. Her eyes lit up. Eagerly, she rushed toward him. She ran past me, pushing me out of the way, and gave him a big hug. Advantage old-boyfriend. It was then I notice he was actually about a half inch taller than me. I was in trouble.

After that humiliating (to me) meeting of the old flames, I spent a forlorn evening alone. She and old boyfriend spent most of the evening catching up on "old times," a discussion in which I could not participate because I did not attend high school with either one of them. To boost my ego, I did go over to one table and tried to convince them I was the star running back on the football team (at a school I never attended). Two of the women at the table finally said, "Oh, yeah, I remember you."

They were kind of cute, but their husbands were sitting right there beside them. Anyway, if I had to start all over, I wanted to do it with a younger woman. Maybe someone three or four months younger than me.

Out of desperation I spent the rest of the evening with Terry. He is a little taller than me, but he is a great dancer. And Mary did not mind sharing him.

At the end of the evening, I managed to reunite with my "wayward" wife. As we pulled into the driveway at

76

home, I commented ruefully, "Well, at least you're coming home with me."

"You were the only one there who knew how to get to my house," she replied without hesitation.

The next morning, I had to talk about the reunion.

"So, I guess I was second choice, huh?"

Janie put her arms around me. She addressed the issue with a parable about her dogs.

"God gave me Tessa. I loved the first Tessa. You know how much I loved the first Tessa, but she died. So, God gave me a second Tessa . . . and do you think I don't love the second Tessa? . . . maybe more than the first."

"So, now I'm fourth choice behind your old boyfriend and two little Yorkies?"

"Don't forget the cats."

Yorkie Number 3

All of Janie's beloved Yorkies finally died and except for a short stay by a rescued Multipoo, we were dogless. As you know from the previous story, Janie loved her Yorkies dearly.

"You know, I would really like another Yorkie," Janie confessed.

"Ain't happenin'."

"But I really want another dog."

"No, my dog-daddy days are long past," I insisted. "No more dogs as long as I'm around. When you see me grab my chest, and this old ticker goes out, and I'm no longer here on this earth, then you can bring a new dog into this house."

"Oh, I hope that doesn't happen soon."

"Why? Because you love me?"

"No, that's not it. I haven't found a new dog yet."

Covid 19 Talk

"I need you to go out and buy me some shredded lettuce."

"I need to shave first."

"No, you don't."

"I am not going out in public with this scruffy beard. I'll look terrible."

"You'll have a mask on."

"Oh, how liberating."

******

Janie handed me a letter to mail.

"What are you getting from the Mayo Clinic?" I asked as I looked at the address.

"I am subscribing to a newsletter. It has all kinds of helpful healthcare hints."

"When it comes to healthcare," I replied, "I don't want hints."

******

"Are you spreading cream cheese on that celery or are you painting the Sistine Chapel?" I asked as Janie slowly spread the cheese.

"Cream cheese should always be handled like a work of art," she replied. "Besides, with this lockdown, what else do I have to do?"

Lions and Tigers and Bears

In 2001, I was flown to the Cleveland Clinic with a hole in my esophagus and massive chest infection after a minor outpatient procedure went terribly wrong. My life was in danger. I underwent an emergency eight-hour-plus operation and came out of surgery with seventeen tubes sticking out of my body. I spent a month in Cleveland, and Janie lived out of a hotel near the hospital at $100 a day plus food.

For four months, my esophagus was literally disconnected from my stomach. I lived off a feed tube and went in and out of the ER and local hospitals several times with other surgeries. On 9/11, 2001 (yes, that 9/11), we were watching for a plane to fly into the hospital. I was back in Cleveland having my stomach reconnected to my esophagus, another eight-hour operation.

My stomach now serves as an esophagus, and I literally have no functioning stomach which helps digest food. I spent several months learning (still learning) how to eat and not get nauseously sick with every meal. Through it all there were two people who were solid rocks for me: Janie and God. At that time, she was nothing less than an Angelic Viking Shield Maiden and Florence Nightingale rolled into one-and God was God. Not once did I ever fear dying, even though I was close on several occasions. Not a single bill went unpaid. Not a single need went unmet.

In time, my full health was restored, I returned to work, I went back to teaching in church, and I watched as my grandkids came along to fill my life with new adventures and memories. Enjoy each day. It is a gift. The chief surgeon had secretly told Janie that life expectancy after this type of surgery was five years. It has been over twenty.

The last thing I remember before going into emergency surgery was a big, tall, black, burly surgeon. He looked more like a football player than a surgeon. As the team of surgeons left, he bent down, gently put his arm around me, leaned close to my ear and said, "We're going to take good care of you." This was more than reassuring words from a surgeon I did not even know. It was a message directly from God. I felt as if this surgeon was an angel sent by God with a message from God himself: "I'm going to take good care of you." In that moment, I had a peace that live or die, indeed, God would take care of me.

I suppose death is our most common fear. I am reminded of what Dorothy said in the Wizard of Oz, "Lions and tigers and bears, oh my!" Lions and tigers and bears? Things to be afraid of? In the movie, they proved to be nothing more than fears produced by the feeble imaginations of Dorothy and her friends. Lions and tigers and bears: nothing more than shadows in a dark forest, faint castings along a dimly lit path. Our fears, also, are but shadows that flee when the light of day dawns, when the Son of God appears. Our fears are but boogie men with no real substance, no real power, and no lasting bite.

And death? The 23rd Psalm says "Though I walk through the valley of the shadow of death, I will fear no evil." Did you catch that? The *shadow of death*, not death itself-merely the shadow of our feared enemy.

I was wrapped in the arms of a skilled and caring surgeon, but in reality he was God's instrument supplying God's reassuring touch. If we are wrapped in the arms of an all-powerful, all-loving God, we will fear no evil, and death will be but a shadow that comes upon our lives and quickly passes. When that shadow flees, we will awaken to a splendor and glory and peace that is beyond description, beyond words, beyond our wildest thoughts and imaginations for we will find ourselves basking in the eternal light and life of God Himself.

More Random Stuff

"Joey's power was out last night," observed Janie. "That happens a lot. Kind of odd for an upscale subdivision."

"The Titanic was upscale, too."

I am particularly proud of this observation. Every once in a while, I have a brilliant insight.

******

After looking at a picture of Janie that was taken about eight years ago, I kept telling her that I like her hair long. I asked if she would go back to that style. I told her the woman in the picture is beautiful. She told me the long hair "ain't happenin'," and I can run off with the woman in the picture if I can find her.

******

Ally, one of our granddaughters, asked Janie, "Nana, how do you have so much money? You and Pawpaw don't work."

"We don't have a lot of money."

"Yes, you do," insisted Ally. "You always have money. Where do you get it?"

"Well,' explained Janie, "Pawpaw was such a bad worker that they now pay him to not come to work."

Note: This was pre-covid19. We were ahead of the times.

Stressing

Some people make stuffing for Thanksgiving. Some people make dressing for the turkey. Janie makes stressing. It is her specialty. She usually does not fix a big meal without stressing. Do not misunderstand. She loves big dinners for the family. Sometimes we have more than twenty people at the table every week. One of the big events is New Year's Day Dinner. While she loves the end result, she does not necessarily enjoy the sometimes-hectic preparation and cooking process. Everything is planned out in detail, not only the menu but also the scheduling for preparing everything. I usually stay out of her way until she needs me, and one never knows when that will be. Sometimes, when the cooking gets intense or behind schedule, she tends to get a little tense. And if she gets tense, the house gets tense, and you know she is cooking up stressing.

New Year's Day Dinner is also our oldest daughter's birthday. Thus, this is a big event, a big production. One year, Janie had been working for hours, and as usual, I was sitting around, waiting for her call for help when I heard this.

"Oh! I think I'm gonna blow a fuse!"

Thinking she is in the process of making stressing, I respond, "Oh, please don't get upset."

"No. Look. I think I'm gonna blow a fuse."

I went into the kitchen and looked at the counter. She had at least six crock pots plugged in. Yes, she really was going to blow a fuse.

Kincaidisms

Here are a few of my famous sayings or Kincaidisms as I like to call them.

- Happiness is found in the reflective moment, not some future event.
- Breathe in the moment, exhale the memories.
- Insanity and Intelligence are on the opposite sides of a Mobius strip.
- Seek a government that will supply your every need, and you will get a government that controls your every wish.
- After fifty-plus years, I can read Janie like a book. Problem is I am still on page one.
- You can photoshop a picture. You cannot photoshop a life.
- Contentment is being at peace with God and yourself regardless of your circumstances.
- The hallmark of humanity is inconsistency.
- Make sure that chip on your shoulder is not your religious beliefs.
- The faster you go, the "behinder" you get.
- Do not be concerned about doing great things. Be concerned about doing good things. Greatness, whatever that is, flows from goodness.

Thrown Under the Bus Romantic Dinner

This is a Fantasy Romantic Dinner. Some of it is true. Some not. I will leave it up to you, the reader, to tell which is which.

One year for our anniversary, we went to a "cozy" restaurant in Pigeon Forge, Tennessee, to celebrate. It was just a small place that seated maybe 500 or 600 people. After a long, long wait, we were seated, and the waitress took our order. After another long wait, the waitress brought our food. She proceeded to place a platter of country fried steak before me. She stepped back and smiled, knowing that I was going to be the tip giver.

I looked down at my entrée and something did not look right.

"I didn't order country fried steak," I said politely with disappointment in my voice.

The waitress looked shocked, apprehensive.

Timidly, she responded, "Yes, you did, I think."

"I thought I ordered pork chops," I said.

My lovely child-bride wife intervened, "No, honey, you ordered country fried steak."

"I did?"

"Yes, you did."

"I thought I ordered pork chop."

"Well, you may have thought pork chop but you said country fried steak," my beloved child-bride wife insisted.

"OK, I'll take it," I conceded with a broken heart and forlorn stomach.

And so, I proceeded to quietly eat my unwanted country fried steak and resume our romantic anniversary conversation when the whole night turned into something like an episode from a bad TV sitcom. A big burly bearded redneck Tennessee chef appeared at our table.

"So, you don't like my country fried steak? No one refuses my country fried steak. I've been working here two weeks, and I know how to make the best country fried steak in Pigeon Forge!" he said confrontationally.

"Yes, I like your country fried steak," I said defensively. "I just didn't order your country fried steak."

"Yes, you did," my precious child-bride wife said. Talk about getting thrown under the bus. I thought she would at least attempt to defend me or rescue me from my precarious situation. But, no, her policy of always telling the truth was putting my life in jeopardy.

"Now apologize to the good chef," she insisted in her most motherly tone, "and to the nice little waitress, and to all these lovely fellow diners before we get thrown out of here."

Embarrassed and threatened by the chef, I pushed my chair back, preparing to apologize. In the process I accidental shoved my plate of country fried steak into the floor. The chef, thinking I was throwing his precious country fried steak at him, suddenly flew into a rage and started chasing me around the dining hall with a meat cleaver.

I don't remember much after that, except that I managed to escape with my life and my hugely-embarrassed but still lovely child-bride wife.

Some Random Family History

True story. Way back in the 1820's my ancestors owned most of the land around Gauley Bridge, West Virginia. A father and son owned a ferry business that took people and things across the Gauley River. The state, Virginia at that time, came along and built a bridge that threatened to put my ancestors out of business. So, like the good, industrious, upstanding, cheapskate businessmen that they were, they did the only thing that could be done. They burned down the bridge. The arson trial followed soon thereafter. They soon discovered you cannot operate a ferry from behind bars.

I cannot say this father-son team were atypical family members. I do, however, remember the words of wisdom that my grandmother gave me before I left home and went out into the world on my own.

"Never forget you're a Kincaid. Act that way."

That always confused me because according to Dad one side of the family was bootleggers and the other half was horse thieves. I was never sure which side of the family we were on and, thus, which side to emulate.

Carpi Diem

Sometimes moments come for, well only for a moment, and you should be ready to breathe in the moment. We were on vacation. I was sitting on the balcony, looking out over the ocean. The quiet water was suddenly interrupted by thousands of fish jumping out of the water as they were being chased by a school of dolphins. This was one reason to come to the beach-to see nature unfold spontaneously before your eyes.

"Come out here and look at all these big fish jumping out there," I called to Janie. "There are thousands of them!"

"I'm reading a book," replied Janie from inside the condo.

"Wow! That was a really big fish. Huge splash. You should come out here and see this!"

"How can I read this book if you keep interrupting me?" she replied.

"This is real life right before your eyes. There are fish out there jumping around and churning up the water and being eaten alive by dolphins! This is a real-life drama and you're reading a book."

"Tell them to wait until I finish this chapter."

Janie has a tough time with the concept of hurry.

A Monkey in the Family Tree

Here is a bit of my family history that has morphed into a morality tale of sorts. Part of it is historically true, and part of it is metaphorically true, but true nonetheless.

Janie and I were helping our daughter with her school social studies project. She was doing research on our family tree. The three of us were spending the day at the West Virginia Archives trying to trace through our genealogy. This was in the days before the Internet, Google, and online genealogy search sites. There among the microfilm, history books, and census records we uncovered a real skeleton in our family's past. This discovery would change forever the way we thought about the Kincaid family. Oh, sure, we had our share of horse thieves and scalawags in the family, but the most devasting revelation of all was the fact that we actually had a monkey in our family tree! After we made that discovery, we stopped our genealogical quest. We really did not want to know about the rest of the family.

The tree-dwelling story goes like this. Back around 1804 my great-great-great-grandparents, James and Mary Kincaid moved from Charlottesville in old Virginia to what is now Greenbrier County, West Virginia. After about five years, they decided to move further west. They had caught the wanderlust that was going around at the time and decided to head deeper into the mountains of Appalachia to seek their fame and fortune. Actually, they cared little for fame and fortune. They just could not take the urban sprawl that was occurring around Greenbrier County in the early 1800's and got a hankering to move out to the suburbs where they could have a creek to call their own.

Following the course of what is now Route 60, they

made their way across Big Sewell Mountain, along the New River Gorge, and settled near what is now Gauley Bridge at the confluence of the New and Gauley Rivers. They found themselves totally lost in the mountains, miles between somewhere and nowhere. It is a place West Virginians call "rye cheer," as in you are over there, but I am "rye cheer." Only then, when they were "rye cheer" in the heart of the mountains did they feel safe enough to stop. Only then did they decide that this was their long sought-after destination-here in the highlands of West Virginia, reminiscent of their Scottish homeland.

James and Mary had but one problem. They had no house to make a home. They also had another problem. Being Kincaids, they were naturally a lazy lot and soon went searching for a quick and easy way to build a house for the winter. Near the river, they found a large, hollow sycamore tree and decided to make that their home. The sycamore, so the story goes, was so large that you could turn inside of it holding a fence rail in your hands. James and Mary cut a hole in the front side of the tree for a window and a small hole in the rear for ventilation. They made beds and trundle beds from poles. In a year or so, they finally got around to building a "real" house by adding a room to that old sycamore tree. Eventually, my great-great-grandfather, Preston Kincaid, was born in the heart of that hollow tree. And so, although I do not believe that humans descended from monkeys, I do know that my ancestors lived like them.

So, James and Mary settled down in their tree house, loving and living, completely unaware that they would soon change the course of history-at least for "rye cheer" in Fayette County, West Virginia. Believe it or not, this couple and their descendants and the families that came after them are directly responsible for West Virginians not liking to wear shoes. Do not misunderstand me. I did not say West Virginians do not wear shoes. I said they do not like to wear shoes.

You see, as the family grew and as a few other people got lost in the mountains and found their way to rye cheer in Fayette County, a magical thing began to happen. They began to grow roots. Real roots. In the beginning, folks thought they had a bad case of heat rash or athlete's feet, but all the itching and scratching, salves and lotions were nary a help. After about a week or two, the little red nubs on the bottom of their feet began to sprout roots-real roots that continued to grow on the soles of their feet-roots that began to grow deep into the rich soil of these mountains. Perhaps there had been something magical in the dirt floor of that sycamore tree-home. Perhaps it was the work of the forest fairies. Who knows? What was certain was the fact that everyone who wandered into Fayette County found themselves confronted with the irresistible urge to pull off their shoes and let those roots on the bottom of their feet grow down into the mother soil.

Now these were common folks, mind you. Responsible folks. Loving folks. They were miners and farmers, housewives and cooks, merchants and carpenters, plumbers and mechanics. Occasionally, they would produce a preacher or two whose roots grew twice as fast as anyone else's. On rare occasions, a lawyer would be born into the community. Now, it was easy to tell if someone was going to be a lawyer: you could find only tiny little nubbins growing on the bottom of his or her feet.

Kids had no problem running barefoot and letting the roots grow wild as they pleased. However, as folks got older, they reluctantly realized that the shoes had to be put on, especially if you were going to spend all day at the mines in the belly of the earth. And yet on occasions, no one, not even Clarence the persnickety old grocer, could resist the urge to pull off his shoes and sink his roots into the warm inviting mountain soil-to stand upon a mountain ridge and know how much he belonged in these hills-to wonder what would happen to his roots if he had to move into the city. Even Farmer Norvel and Preacher Mac were a common sight down by the creek, pretending to be fishing while all the time they were really watering their roots in the cool waters of the community fishing hole.

After the Civil War, a highfaluting Boston doctor came to Fayette County. His name was Doctor Reginald D. Bailey, III, MD, and his goal was to become world famous by curing the Fayette County Root Rot as he called it. He bristled when people called him Reggie. He bristled even more when they called him Doc Bailey. It was Doctor Reginald D. Bailey, III, MD, thank you. His project ended as failure of sorts. After a couple of months, he caught the Fayette County Root Rot himself. He tried all kinds of cures, but nothing worked. Eventually, he went back to Boston, sold his practice, and moved to Fayette County. After moving into his new house, he proudly hung a sign on the front porch that read, "Doc Bailey, Family Doctor." That is what Fayette County Root Rot can do to you. It prevents you from being pompous.

Legend has it that Big Bill Bellows, our representative in the state legislature in the late 1800s, would take a box of Fayette County soil with him to the state capitol. Whenever the work began to wear on him, he would whip off his shoes and soak his roots in that box for a few minutes to soothe his soul. That box of soil also came in handy when he wanted to deliver an impassioned speech. Standing barefoot in that box of Fayette County soil, his roots well-nourished and strong, he would lift his voice to the heights of oratory, shaking the very foundations of that great hall. Folks say there never was and never will be again an orator like Barefoot Big Bill Bellows. Of course, that is according to legend, and you do not have to believe it if you think that this is a little farfetched. Personally, I think all politicians should be required to deliver all of their speeches barefooted, standing in a box of dirt. Some humility and honesty might be added to what they have to say.

Anyway, throughout the years, the folks in Fayette County were growing roots on their feet, which made it extremely uncomfortable in shoes. The Civil War came and passed, and the roots continued to grow. The great expansion West came and passed, and the roots grew deeper still. All through World War I and the Roaring Twenties, through the Great Depression and World War II, you guessed it, the roots grew deeper still. And then shortly after World War II, I was born. My parents rejoiced. I was not going to be a lawyer. I had roots, too.

At first, the roots did not bother me. I simply did not pay much attention to them. After all, everyone else had them. However, when I went away to college out of state and discovered that I was different, my roots began to cause me concern. I encountered a lot of people who did not have roots, and some of them even made fun of mine. I remember coming home at spring break and talking with Pappy about it. Now, Pappy was not my pappy, but everyone called him that, even his wife and mother called him Pappy. He was an old, wise, weather-worn mountaineer to whom everyone went to for advice. Folks considered him to be an oracle of sorts. There was not anything about life or these mountains that Pappy did not know about.

When I asked him about my roots, this is what he told me.

"Oh, I can tell ya how to get rid of 'em easy enough, but don't ya know, son, that it's those roots that help you stand tall to give ya a steady eye to better see the path ahead? Don't ya know, son, that it's those roots that keep yer pace slow and deliberate, instead of runnin' hither and yon with every whim of the road? And don't ya know, boy, that when the storms of life come along and the opposition presses in against ya, that it's those roots that help ya stand firm and strong without being broken in the battle? Now, I'm not much fer tellin' folks what to do, but if I were you, son, I wouldn't turn my back on one of the greatest earthly gifts that God has given ya. Now, in the great scheme of things, I may not count fer much, boy-but *I do know my roots*."

I must confess to you that my roots are still there. To many people they have been a well-kept secret. From time to time, I would trim them a bit, especially when I had a three-piece-suit meeting at corporate headquarters which required keeping my shoes on for most of the day and half the evening. But they are still there. You cannot remove decades of growth in just a few years-perhaps not in a lifetime. And I must confess that nothing feels better than to kick off my shoes on a hot summer's day and let those roots seek out the nourishment needed from the mountains I love.

Well, that is the story, believe it or not. West Virginians do not like wearing shoes because of their roots -real, deep, abiding roots.

The Epiphany

This was such a watershed, serendipitous epiphany for me that I have to share it with you. It has nothing and yet everything to do with my marriage. It may well be a parable about something important, but I will leave that to you to figure out.

Years ago, late at night, I was coming home from a business trip. I was on a plane from Newark to Pittsburgh. I was mentally exhausted. As I gazed out the window, I spotted an unusually bright star in the clear autumn sky. My mind became transfixed on that star as I wondered what might be out there-probably thousands, maybe millions of light years away. Could there, perhaps, be people just like us living on some Earth-like world orbiting that far away point of light?

As we sped through the night, I contemplated what life could be like out there. Were there people just like us orbiting that far away star with the same hopes and dreams and fears? Was there someone out there gazing back at me at that very moment, perhaps pondering the same ideas? As the other passengers slept, I felt a peaceful calm come over me as I began to feel a cosmic connection-an intimate union with the universe, so to speak. My very being was being absorbed into the very fabric of space and time. A star child was gaining universal consciousness.

And then, as the plane began to descend into the greater Pittsburgh area, I discovered that my cosmic connection-my soul-sister star-was a light on the end of the left wing.

Random Stuff Again

"Today we have to blah, blah, blah blah . . . da-blah."

"What?" I asked as I continued to type on my laptop, only half-hearing what she said.

"I said, we need to waa, waa, waa, waa . . . da-blah."

Me, still typing, "What?"

"Just say OK."

"OK."

"Good. I'm glad you agree. Now, blah, blah, blah . . "

******

I smiled as I pushed the button to open the new garage door that I had installed all by myself.

"It works! Aren't you impressed?"

"Not really," Janie replied. "It's supposed to work."

Ah, the spirit of Shania Twain lives on.

******

One day I came strolling through the house wearing new blue jeans, my sleeves rolled up to my elbows, and collar turned up in the back while sporting a cool set of shades.

"Get a load of this, babe. I'm doin' my James Dean impersonation."

"James Dean is dead."

******

"My ribs are sore. They really hurt when I breathe," I complained.

"Don't breathe."

Backseat Baptists

We sit in the back row at church. I will tell you why. Years ago, the church we attended held week-long revivals. Janie played the piano one year for the revival, and we sat on the front row. The guest evangelist had preached his heart out but got absolutely no altar call responses. On the last day of the revival son Joe, about ten at the time, had to go to the bathroom. He quietly got up and walked out the back of the sanctuary. When he returned, the evangelist was in the middle of his altar call, but he was still getting no responses.

Son Joe was quietly walking down the center aisle to his seat when the evangelist saw him and got excited. He had finally gotten someone to respond to his sermons even if it was a ten-year-old kid.

"That's right, son. Come on down and get saved!" he called from the pulpit.

This sudden attention shocked Son Joe. He was petrified. He stopped in his tracks right in the middle of the aisle. He had already been saved and did not see the need to do it again.

"Come, on down, son. Don't you want to get saved?"

Even at age ten, never ask Son Joe a question if you are not prepared for an honest answer. He is too much like his mother. You will get a straight-up honest answer.

"No," replied Son Joe.

"You don't want to be saved?"

"No. I did that last year. I just want to go sit with my mommy."

The evangelist left town, devastated.

On another earlier occasion, Son John was acting up, so I took him by the hand to lead him out into the lobby. As we were walking toward the back door, Son John was calling in a loud voice, "Help me! Help Me! Somebody pray for me!"

And that is why we sit on the back row.

A Fractured Fairy Tale

Once upon a time, a fairy godmother arranged for Cinderella to go to the Royal Ball. She had a wonderful time dancing with the prince, but had to leave before the stroke of midnight, otherwise she and her carriage horses would turn into avocados or something like that. As she rushed away before the stroke of midnight, one of her shoes came off. In her haste preparing Cinderella for her last-minute trip to the ball, the fairy godmother gave her shoes that were a half size too large, and thus the oversized shoe came off as she ran away.

To the prince's dismay, she disappeared into the night, leaving only her shoe as evidence of her identity. Not to be deterred and using his royal privileges, the royal prince sent the Royal Shoe-Tryer-On-Guy out into the kingdom with the shoe to find the girl of his dreams. Obviously, he had had too much to drink at the Royal Ball and could not remember what she looked like and was too lazy to go and search for her himself.

As chance would have it, the Royal Shoe-Tryer-On-Guy came to the house beside where Cinderella lived. There he found a woman whose foot fit the shoe perfectly. As chance would have it, her foot was exactly one-half size larger than Cinderella's. The Royal Shoe-Tryer-On-Guy did not think this seventy-five-year-old woman with droopy eyelids and various other sagging body parts was the girl of the prince's dreams. But, hey, the shoe fit.

So, declaring victory after finding the first foot that fit (even with a copious number of corns and bunions), the Royal Shoe-Tryer-On-Guy took the woman to the prince. Foolishly trusting the evidence of the shoe, that is seeing that the shoe fit, he promptly married the woman with the droopy eyelids and various other sagging body parts. It never crossed his mind that the elderly lady looked nothing like the girl at the ball. He also found out later that she could not dance and had great difficulty climbing stairs.

The prince and the saggy-eyed lady lived relatively happily ever after. Not much ever after because of her age, but happily ever after nonetheless. At times he secretly wondered if he had married the right woman, but divorce was forbidden in fairy-tale land.

Cinderella, on the other hand, fired her incompetent fairy godmother for bad planning and went back to work for her cruel stepmother, sweeping floors and doing laundry. She also ate her carriage horses which had changed back into over-ripe avocados. The leftover glass slipper was used as a very nice petunia planter.

The moral of the story: Do not drink too much at the ball. You may not be able to identify the real girl of your dreams. Do not trust the shoe, even if it fits. If you want to find the girl of your dreams look for her yourself. And finally, do not go unprepared to a big event at the last minute. Something will go wrong, at the worst possible moment.

On a related subject, I saw an ad for a dating service recently. You simply filled out a bio-sheet online, and the dating service did the rest. They matched your profile to the person of your dreams. They arranged for the first date. They told you where to go on the date. They even told you what to wear and what to talk about. I guess the days of do-it-yourself dating are long gone.

Home Alone Dreams

"No grandkids this morning?" I asked.

"Nope."

"You know, if we didn't have grandkids, we could cuddle in bed every morning until ten."

"No. My hands would fall asleep and my legs would cramp up. I hate when that happens."

Me (ignoring her complaints), "And then we could get up and go for a long walk in the woods."

"No. I'd get sweaty and bitten by insects-and my shoes would get dirty."

Me (still ignoring her complaints), "And then we'd come back and have some tea and crumpets on the veranda."

"I don't like crumpets," she said, "and we don't have a veranda."

"I love it when you play along with my fantasies."

"You're welcome."

Bringing Home the Bacon

Recently, Janie brought tears to my eyes by reminding me about the little things in life that are truly important. I called her and told her I was not buying any more bacon because it was becoming too expensive. I told her that it now cost over $10,000 a ton. She told me that God had blessed us with independent wealth and as long as we did not have to sell the yacht or Lear jet, or mortgage our mountain chalet we would continue to buy bacon-just maybe not by the ton.

Run Away with Me

One morning at breakfast, I asked, "Have you ever thought of running away with me and living on some secluded island?"

"No. I have too many responsibilities."

"You're supposed to be romantic and say yes."

"You want me to lie?" And then she smiles and says in her most soft, romantic voice, "I plan to stay right here at this kitchen island and grow old with you."

"Is that our only option?"

It Is Good to Be Wanted

I came down to the kitchen one morning and gave Janie a big hug. Then, I told her, "I love it when you hug me in the morning. When you just hold me. It lets me know I am not alone in the world, that I'm not abandoned in the universe. It tells me I don't have to depend on some periodic alien abduction to feel significant."

Janie, shaking her head, "You are a nutcase."

The Dangers of Doughnuts

We were in Pigeon Forge for a softball tournament. Sometimes, our granddaughter Maddie would play four or five games in one day-with catcher's equipment on-in 90-degree heat. One morning, we were in the car, headed for the ballfield after eating only doughnuts for breakfast.

"I didn't eat an egg like I usually do. I need to get some protein," Janie observed.

Our granddaughter, Ally, was with us.

"Why, Nana?" she asked.

Janie launched into a long explanation of "absorption of carbs" and "metabolism," etc. And then she added, "And if I don't get my protein, I get grumpy."

"Ally," I said, attempting to clarify what Janie was saying about a proper diet, "what she means is her fangs come out and her ears get pointy."

I could see in the rear-view mirror Ally's eyes get really big and wide.

"Oh, that" Ally said knowingly.

"Yeah," admitted Janie. "Not a pretty sight."

Christmas Angels
Mid 1990s

Here is a little Christmas story about when the kids were still at home and our oldest daughter was in college.

I knew I was in trouble. After twenty-some years of marriage, you have that sixth sense that tells you when things are about to head south. Janie had been pouring over a bunch of papers for more than an hour. She had them spread out all over the dining room table and was deeply engrossed in the paperwork. Whenever she did that, I always knew something momentous was on the horizon. To make matters worse, she had a calendar. That could only mean one thing. She was about to announce the family's Christmas schedule in minute, minute-by-minute detail.

Your family does not maintain a Christmas schedule? Consider yourselves blessed. With a hyperactive family of six, a schedule was an absolute necessity at our house, but sometimes Janie took it to extremes. Now, most people will tell you that if you want something organized, let my wife handle it. No detail is too small. No job is too large. I am not bragging, folks, but it seems to me she always knows exactly what to do. Every angle is covered. Every possibility is planned. That is usually because she has spent a lot of time and energy worrying about everything that might go wrong and thus is ready for any contingency no matter how remote. However, when it came to our family's Christmas schedule, I think sometimes she went a little overboard.

"Mr. Kincaid, can you come in here to the dining room for a minute?"

Anytime she was serious, she called me "Mr. Kincaid." At other times, it was "Hey you" or "Honey." On rare occasions. it was "John" or "Johnny." Most of the time at this stage of our marriage, however, I was never spoken to directly at all. She usually communicated through the kids as though I was not even in the room. It was always "Your father" this or "Your daddy" that. Not only did she speak in that manner but the kids did also.

Let me give you an example. Now you must keep in mind that I am usually in the same room with these people.

Wife Jane: "Joey, hasn't your father helped you with your math yet?"

Son Joey: "No, Mom, he hasn't."

Wife Jane: "Did he tell you that he was too busy?"

Son Joey: "No. He said he would do it later."

Wife Jane: "Do you think I can get your dad to help me clean up the kitchen tonight?"

Daughter Kimberly: "Mom, can Daddy watch Home Improvement with me tonight?"

Wife Jane: "I don't know, dear. Your father is a very busy man."

Son John: "Mom, can Dad give me twenty bucks for a date tonight?"

Wife Jane: "Now, son, you know your father isn't made out of money."

Son John: "I don't know, Mom. I saw something green behind his ear this morning."

And so, the conversations go. Generally, when they begin speaking in that manner, I simply tune out the entire conversation. After all, they are not talking to me, they are talking about me. When people talk about you, it is called gossip, and my mother had taught me to never listen to gossip. Usually, the end of the "your daddy" conversations ended with someone saying, "I think Dad needs a hearing aid." Well, maybe he does, but he has always heard that last comment.

But I digress.

I had been formally summoned to the planning table.

104

It mattered not that I was watching the fourth quarter of a Chicago Bulls-New York Knicks basketball game. It mattered not that Michael Jordan was on the verge of scoring fifty points. The Great Organizer had reached her verdict, and I was expected to concur with her conclusions.

"Can you give me ten minutes?" I called, pleadingly down the hall, knowing full well what the answer would be.

"I don't have ten minutes, Hon. I've got a meeting at church at five."

At least she called me "Hon." That was a good sign.

"Oh, well," I said as Michael drove the baseline for a slam dunk. "Be there in a second."

Remember, this was the days before DVRs. No record options. Maybe this will not take that long, and I can return to the game I told myself. But I knew as soon as I left the room, I would never see that game again. Ewing picked up his fifth foul, and the Knicks called a timeout. A commercial about beer-drinking frogs came on. This I could miss. I hurried down the hall to stand at the dining room door.

"Come in, sit down. I need to show you something."

"Sit down" was another sure catch phrase. When she said "sit down" that meant she wanted my full cooperation and attention. I sat down at the dining room table, and she handed me a calendar.

"Now this is very important, and I want you to pay close attention," she began.

You would have thought she was talking to a six-year-old. I can pay attention when I want to. The only problem is that most of the time I do not want to. Most of the time my mind is like a hyperactive fourth-grader, wandering and darting from idea to idea without much thought or concern about what is going on around me in the outside world. Some folks believe I am a deep thinker who gets lost in his thoughts. Well, I do get lost in my thoughts, but not because my thoughts are so deep. They just take so many twists and turns that I forget where I started or how I got to the thought at hand. I have considered leaving mental bread crumbs to mark my path, but that only confuses me more. Sometimes people comment on what a studious thinker I am. They would be surprised to know how superficial most of my thought processes really are. Not paying attention is one of my great faults, but frankly, I have not been able to sit down and think long enough about a solution to the problem.

But I digress.

Janie was requesting-no, demanding my full attention. From the TV down the hallway, I could hear the basketball crowd screaming loudly. I wondered what the score was now, and who had just made a spectacular play.

"Yes, sir," I said. I always teased her by calling her "sir" in situations like this.

"I'm not a sir," she said curtly, "and don't you start that goofing around like you always do. This is serious, Mr. Kincaid. I need your full, complete and undivided attention. OK?"

"OK," I said. I had no other safe alternative.

"This is our family Christmas schedule," she announced, pointing a red pen at a cluttered calendar. (real picture)

"Do we have to go to this much detail?" I asked, looking at a calendar cluttered with red marks, circles, and notes. I am not much of a detail person. I like to work with the big picture. Besides, there is an old saying: "The devil is in the details." I thought as

106

Christians we were supposed to avoid the devil.

"Look," she announced, "we all have church activities-plays, cantatas, practices, special services, social events-high school activities, middle school activities, elementary school activities, community events, piano lessons, gymnastic lessons, basketball practice, more piano lessons, dance lessons, doctor's appointments, your work schedule, Christmas caroling, Christmas cards, candy making, package wrapping, visits by relatives, visits to relatives, visits to friends and neighbors, parties, trips to see the decorations and lights, and shopping trips.

"Besides that, we've got to clean the house. And I don't mean clearing a path through the hallway. I don't mean your regular vacuuming and dusting. I mean deep cleaning. Your mother is coming next weekend, and the house has got to be spotless."

I wondered why the house had to be clean for my mother and not for my dad. We never had to clean the house because dad was coming next weekend.

"And when your mother gets here, remember you're not her little boy any longer, so don't act like it. You're a grown man with kids, not a little boy."

Gee, now she was taking all of the fun out of Christmas.

"Is that all?" I asked, while wondering how many points Michael had by that time.

Janie looked disturbed. "You don't take all this seriously, do you? You don't really understand me, do you?"

"Yes, I do," I said defensively. I lied. Forgive me Lord, but that was the safest thing to do at the time. I lied. I really didn't understand why Christmas had to be so hectic. I didn't understand why we could not plan a more leisurely Christmas.

"Look," Janie continued, "we have decorations to put

up, and we still haven't found the wreath we lost last year that goes on the front door. And I have also got cookies to bake, and candy to make, and fruitcakes and pies and other things to cook. We have got dogs to groom, presents to wrap, letters to write, cars to clean, and Maggie will be home from college with a car load of dirty clothes to wash, and" She stopped and sighed. "Well, it's all here on the schedule."

I did not want to look, but I did anyway just to pacify her.

"And what do you want me to do?" I asked.

"I want you to help me get through this any way you can. I want you to find solutions. I want you to be creative. I want you to be cooperative. And I want you to stay out of my way."

I liked that last one. I knew how to stay out of the way. I could even arrange a two-week business trip right in the middle of December. That would get me "out of the way," but how was I supposed to help if I did that?

"OK," I said lamely. I pretended to study the calendar, but in truth it was so overwhelming that I could not take any of it in. In my imagination, all I could see was a daily 16-hour marathon from now until Christmas. Already I was exhausted. Then, I noticed that according to the calendar, I was already behind schedule.

"Um, Janie, I don't think you have enough bathroom breaks."

"Whattaya mean?" she asked, grabbing the calendar from my hand. "I didn't put any on the schedule."

"That's just it," I teased. "No potty breaks for five weeks won't do."

She looked at me and frowned. "Oh, you never take me seriously, do you?"

"Yes, yes, I do. It's just that, well, I think you take all of this too seriously. I mean, where's the time for quiet reflection and spontaneity?"

"Right here," she said, pointing to the calendar.

"Where?" I asked incredulously.

"Right here. December 12th at 8pm: 'Quiet family get together for spontaneous seasonal meditation.'"

My loving child-bride wife had obviously not taken Logic 101. There is no such thing as planned spontaneity.

"But what if there's a super sale down at Kmart that night?" I asked, trying to inject some humor into the conversation.

"We'll just reschedule our family meeting for the 18th," she said seriously without a hint of hesitation.

"OK," I challenged, "what would you like for me to do now?"

"Right now, just leave me alone. I have to get ready to go to church."

Let me tell you younger guys what your wife means when she tells you to leave her alone. She means you are supposed to be a mind reader. She does not mean to leave her completely alone. She just means to leave her alone until she needs you to fasten a necklace or something like that. Here is where the mind reading comes in. When she does need you to fasten that necklace, she expects you to be right there. Immediately. Typically, however, you have been told no more than two minutes earlier to leave her alone. So, are you supposed to actually leave her alone or leave her alone until she needs help? And when do you know when she is going to need help? How far away should you be to leave her alone and be ready to help at the same time at a moment's notice? These are questions of great mystery and consequence that men have pondered throughout the ages. You can be assured that over time your mind reading skills will improve, but they will never be perfect.

But I digress.

Surprisingly, the schedule worked flawlessly for several days. I was on my best behavior and tried diligently to pay attention to the hubbub surrounding me. We found the missing wreath. It was under an old overcoat on my side of the closet. We got the house cleaned and decorated just in time for my mother's arrival. Dad came too, but remember, he doesn't count. We even made it through the first weekend of activities.

One day, I came in and dutifully checked the schedule. For Janie's sake, I was determined to make this work. We have always been at odds with each other concerning our basic approach to life. My philosophy has always been to worry about as few things as possible, no need to clutter your mind with all of that serious thinking. Her philosophy has been to worry about as many things as possible. Her explanation is that if you worry about all of the bad things that can happen, they won't. So far, I must admit, she has been right. Over the years we have constructed a working, and I must say successful, coalition. She encourages me to be more serious and responsible, and I encourage her to be more relaxed and spontaneous.

But I digress.

I checked the calendar for the day and noticed a task that read "Wrap orphan gifts." I did not know any orphans that needed gifts, so finding Janie in the bedroom wrapping presents, I asked her what that was all about.

"It's these gifts right here," she said with a smile.

"But who are the orphans?" I asked.

"There aren't any. That's just a figure of speech."

"I don't get it," I said. That was not unusual. There were a lot of things that went on in my house that I did not understand.

"The children's Christmas program is tonight at church," she explained. "Each child is supposed to bring a gift to put under the Christmas tree. The gifts are then redistributed to all of the kids."

"Sounds simple, but who are these gifts for?"

"Look. If someone forgets or doesn't know to bring a gift, what happens?"

"They get left out of the gift giving."

"Right. Or worse yet, someone who brought a gift gets left out of the gift giving. In either case, how will that person feel, especially if they're five or six years old?"

"Left out," I said.

"Right."

There was a look on her face that told me she was speaking from personal experience.

"And one of the worst feelings in the world is to be left out at Christmas."

She carefully attached a bow to the package she was wrapping.

"No one should come to church and leave feeling they have been left out or neglected. No one."

"So, you take these extra gifts to church just in case someone doesn't bring a gift."

I was humbled. I would never have thought of that.

"What made you think of doing this?" I asked.

"Oh, I've done it every year."

"You have? Really? I didn't know."

"That's because you don't pay attention. If you paid attention, you'd know what has to be done."

"Do people know you do this?"

"No. Why should they?"

"Just curious."

I could see behind that facade of rigid organization lay a heart of love and true concern, an unselfish spirit. As a society, we often speak of every child being important, but here was a concrete demonstration of that concern. Here was someone who was showing her faith by her actions. Here, I thought, was a real Christmas angel. Her gifts would be given in secret. No one would know what she had done, but someone would be touched by her thoughtfulness.

We took the extra presents to church that evening and quietly, without fanfare, placed them under the tree. At the end of the evening, all of the gifts were gone. Maybe a detailed master schedule was of value after all.

Daughter Maggie's call from college, however, changed everything. She was working as a Resident Advisor or RA for the university. RAs are responsible for maintaining peace and order in the dormitories. They are charged with enforcing university rules and policies, and they are to act as advisors to the other students on their floor. In exchange for all of this, the university gives the RA free room and board. All in all, not a bad deal if the fellow inmates behave.

"I've got some bad news," Maggie said as we listened over the phone. "I won't be home for Christmas."

"How come?" Janie asked with distress clearly evident in her voice.

"Because," Maggie explained, "some of the RAs have to stay in the dorms over Christmas break. It's part of our contract, and it's my turn."

"How come?" I asked. "Isn't the campus closed over the holidays?"

"Yes, but some of us have to stay and keep a watch on things."

"You mean that you're gonna be all alone in the dorm over Christmas?" Janie asked.

"No. There will be other RAs on other floors."

"But you'll be all alone on your floor?" I asked.

"Yes, I'm afraid so."

Now I was the one who was doing the worrying. I had visions of a lonely and deserted midtown campus. I had visions of a lonely and deserted dormitory. I had visions of my lovely daughter riding a lonely and deserted elevator to the twelfth floor and emerging to a lonely and deserted hallway. Except that hallway would not be lonely and deserted. There would be a madman, a rapist, a brutal serial killer waiting for her. She would be alone and defenseless against his attack. All of that flashed through my mind in a split second.

"You're not staying there alone," I insisted. "You're coming home for the holidays."

"Dad, it's OK. I won't be alone. There will be other RAs in the building. And there will be security guards in the main lobby. I'll be all right."

"But you'll be alone on your floor."

"Dad, I'm a big girl. I can take care of myself. I'll be all right."

"And you'll miss Christmas with the family," Janie interjected.

"No, not completely. I'm close enough that I can come home a couple of times a week during the day."

"So, it's OK for you to be gone during the day, but they want you there all alone at night."

Now I was even more concerned for her safety.

"Dad, they lock the doors at night. OK? Besides, I'm trained in self-defense. Now don't worry about it."

Look who she was telling not to worry.

"Well, there goes my schedule," Janie exclaimed.

"We'll work something out, Mom. Besides, I'm working on an idea for something special. I'll let you know in a day or two. OK?"

"OK," Janie said sadly.

"You take care of yourself," I admonished.

"I will, Dad. Now don't worry. I love you."

"Love you too," Janie and I said together.

"Bye."

I came into the kitchen where Janie had been using the cordless phone (a modern miracle at the time). She smiled

113

at me broadly and shook her head.

"What's that for?" I asked.

"It's about time you started worrying about something."

Yeah, maybe it was.

Our family had always been together at Christmas, especially Christmas Eve. I was not sure how we all were going to handle the separation from an emotional point of view. I realized that Maggie's absence actually signified something deeper in the dynamics of our family relationships. She was no longer our "little girl," but a grown woman. I knew that more and more the boundaries of our family would be stretched. The old close-knit family structure was slowly being dismantled by time, and we would have to find a way to construct a new and lasting framework. In other words, folks, skipping all the psycho-babble, Janie and I were getting older.

Maggie called the next night to discussed the situation.

"I've got a great idea," Maggie offered. "Why don't you all come down to the dorm for Christmas Eve?"

"What can we do down there?" I asked.

"The same thing we always do. Mom can bring down all the cookies and candy and ham and cheese and stuff. And you all can bring some presents to open, and we can play some music, and Dad can read the Bible story, and -"

"I don't know," said Janie, obviously worrying about the logistics of the whole operation. "Where can we do this? Certainly not in your room."

"We can use the lounge off of the lobby on the ground floor."

"The one with all the big windows?" I asked.

"Yes, that's the one."

Great, I thought. That dorm was on the busiest street in the town. Everyone in the whole city would see our every move, even Jack the Ripper.

"Well, maybe," said Janie. "I'll have to think about it."

"Oh, Mom, it'll be OK. Besides, there's another reason why I want you to come."

"What's that?"

"There's another RA. His name is Kyle-"

"You're not engaged or anything like that, are you?" I asked nervously. My budget was not ready for an expensive wedding.

"No, Kyle is just a friend. He has to stay here just like me except his family lives far away, so he won't see them at all this Christmas. I thought if you all came down, we could invite him to join us. That way he won't feel so left out and alone on Christmas Eve."

I looked at Janie and smiled. I knew that clinched the deal. Maggie had the heart of her mother.

"If that's the case," said Janie, "we'll be down. Just make sure it's OK with Kyle."

"No problem," said Maggie. "I've already talked with him, and he's looking forward to seeing all of us."

"You mean you told him we were coming before you talked with me?" Janie asked incredulously.

No one ever did that. At Christmas, she was the Master Scheduler. All activities had to be cleared through her.

"I knew you'd say yes, so be down here at five. I've already cleared everything with the security guards."

I smiled again. My daughter was more like my wife than either of them realized-apparently all organized, business-like, and tough as nails on the outside, but all heart on the inside.

* * * * * * * * *

"Are we going for the evening, or are we staying for a week?"

I was looking at the mind-boggling array of stuff that

115

was hanging out of the trunk of my car.

"It's just food, presents, and decorations."

"Decorations?   Do we really need to take decorations?"

Janie gave me that you-are-not-paying-attention-to-detail look again.

"Yes, you need decorations. What would Christmas Eve be without decorations?"

"Sorry. I wasn't thinking."

"That's right. You weren't thinking."

She switched to her now-I'm-going-to-give-you-a-little-good-behavior-speech expression.

"Look. We're going down to the university tonight to be with our oldest daughter and Kyle Whoeverheis. I want this to be an enjoyable evening, so I want you to pay attention and stop asking silly questions. OK?"

"OK," I said, wondering what the silly questions were that I had been asking.

"What's this for?" I asked, pointing to a duffel bag lying on top of the heap.

She looked at me and immediately I knew I had asked a silly question.

"It's our emergency kit just in case we get stranded in bad weather."

I looked up at a clear sky.

"It's 45 degrees. The weather report says it's not going to snow for three or four more days. Besides, you'll never get all of this stuff into the trunk."

"The weather report has been wrong before. You never know when something is going to develop. You should always be prepared."

As we struggled to get the trunk shut, I refrained from asking any more questions or making any suggestions. I knew sooner or later Janie would get everything to fit. She always did. She was also the Master Packer. When the family was younger, she set the unofficial world's record for the most vacation junk stuffed into a family sedan-six suitcases, four kids, two adults, a play pen, a cooler, a stroller, three bags of groceries, two bags of diapers, a porta-potty, an emergency kit, a watermelon, a half bushel of tomatoes, three cantaloupes, four folding chairs, a beach umbrella, a lifetime supply of toothpicks, and one large wicker chair bought at a huge discount.

But I digress.

At long last, the trunk was packed and shut, and our three children were safely tucked into the back seat. They were all growing bigger and the backseat was cramped, but they still fit. Barely. Finally, we were on our way to our Christmas Eve rendezvous.

Maggie was waiting excitedly for us when we arrived at the dorm. We proceeded to unload the car.

"Do we really need all of this?" she whispered to me as we struggled with unloading all of the paraphernalia.

"Don't ask," I warned.

We carried everything into the lounge and began to setup. As the younger children put up decorations, Janie and Maggie were busy preparing the food table. And me? I was dutifully guarding the large window facing the street. I inspected each car that stopped for the red light. I was diligently looking for any suspicious character who might want to crash our little party.

"Where's Kyle?" I asked as I continued to survey the traffic outside.

"Oh, he's in his room. Just a minute and I'll go call him."

Maggie went down the hall to the guard station and picked up the phone. A few minutes later, the elevator doors opened. Kyle emerged into the hallway. His shoulders were broad and his muscular arms gracefully propelled the wheelchair in which he sat.

117

"Hey, everyone, this is Kyle," said Maggie.

We all shook his hand and introduced ourselves, and he thanked us for inviting him to our humble celebration.

"Think nothing of it," said John William, our oldest son. "We need all the help we can get eating all this food."

"I think I know where we should start," I said, nodding toward the food table.

It was not long before everyone had their plate over-flowing with goodies. As we ate, Maggie popped a tape into her boom box, and instantly we were serenaded with Christmas carols.

A tradition in our family was (and still is) to open one present on Christmas Eve. Since this was Christmas Eve, Janie had brought along everything we needed. Everyone had a present to open. Everyone except Kyle. He had two. Janie had brought one for him, and Maggie had also. I would not have expected anything less.

A little later I had retreated to a sofa for some quiet contemplation. As I surveyed the scene, something simple, yet profound piqued my attention. Janie and Kimberly were at the food table, searching for a final few morsels of party snacks. Maggie was changing the tape in the boom box while John, Joey and Kyle huddled in intense conversation. They were probably discussing the latest video game or sci-fi movie.

I quietly watched their conversation from afar. John William turned and said something to Maggie, and she tossed her head back and laughed. Janie giggled and soon everyone was laughing and pointing at John William. I had been so engrossed in my own thoughts that I had apparently missed the best joke of the evening. John William beamed because of the attention, and Joey curled up on a couch in laughter. Little Kim snorted, and that set off another round of furious laughter. This simple scene suddenly invoked in me a realization of something important. Hugely important.

My family truly enjoyed being in each other's company. They really wanted to be together.

I watched as they were laughing, and talking, and joking around. Now John William was doing one of his movie character impersonations, Chewbacca from Star Wars, and everyone else was engrossed in his performance.

At that moment, a little word crept into my consciousness: love. My family actually loved one another. They actually liked buying gifts for one another. They genuinely, at a deep level, cared for one another. They truly enjoyed each other's company. Now that was something you could not plan or schedule, I thought. That was something more akin to a miracle. I thought of all the families in turmoil, those struggling just to get by, those fractured by failure, those devastated by disappointments. How was I and my family so fortunate? Why had I lucked into such a family? As I continued to survey the scene, I realized that here were my Christmas angels-my family. These were the only Christmas gifts that I would ever really need.

And then I realized something earth shattering. A huge paradigm shift. None of this had happened by accident. Janie had planned it all along, years ago, probably in the middle of our first kiss. This is what she wanted when she said, "I do." A family of her own, one she never fully had as a child, and she allowed me to be a part of building it. Somehow, she had planted the seeds for this very night over twenty years ago. Right then and there I thanked God for her foresight.

My serendipitous thoughts were interrupted by the phrase "Your father needs a hearing aid." That was my cue to cease my daydreaming and rejoin the real world.

"I do not," I said defensively. "I know exactly what's been going on." For once, I knew exactly what I was talking about.

119

Later, when the devotions were done, and the gathering was over, and the evening was spent, we started packing up to leave. After delivering a load of stuff to the car, John William came back with something white covering his head and shoulders.

"It's snowing like crazy out there!" he exclaimed.

"What?" I said in astonishment. "It can't be. The weatherman said -"

"When are you ever going to listen to me?" Janie scolded. "The weather forecast is never right. Now you know why I packed that emergency kit."

We finished loading up the car and bid Maggie and Kyle goodnight. Kyle promised to keep a close watch on things there at the dorm. Somehow, I knew he would.

As we drove through the night with the snow falling heavily, everyone lapsed into silence. Kim and Joey dozed off to sleep in the back seat. John William, exhausted from his comic performances for the evening, sat quietly. In a few hours, it would be Christmas. We had successfully made it through another action-packed season. Tomorrow we would open our remaining presents and relax. Tomorrow, even for Janie, there was no schedule to keep.

The snow fell furiously on the windshield, and the slush-covered pavement muffled the usual road noises. The car seemed to be gliding effortlessly along the road toward home.

"You know," Janie said, "what we need is a bigger car."

"How's that?" I asked.

"We need a car that will hold the whole family."

"No, we don't. We don't need a bigger car. We need another car. Son John is driving, and Joey will be driving in a few months. What we need is a second car."

"No," insisted Janie. "We need a bigger car. One that will hold all six of us."

120

"Why do you say that?"

"If I told you, you'd think I was worrying too much."

"Try me."

"Well, we need a bigger car just in case there's a nuclear war or something like that."

She hesitated.

"Well, go on," I urged.

"Well, if we had a bigger car, we could all get in it and head for the hills. I know this secluded little place up in the mountains not far from here . . ."

Now that is what I call really planning ahead. She probably has the next thirty years all mapped out.

The End?

I hope you have enjoyed this little excursion into just some of my conversations with a smart, hip and metaphorically-hot married woman. What started with a chance glance at a young girl in a miniskirt evolved into a life-long conversation which has continued for over fifty years of "becoming one flesh." It is true that the marriage ceremony makes you "one flesh" in a legal sense, but becoming "one flesh" in daily life takes a lot longer than twenty minutes.

Allow me to leave you with what I wrote some forty-five years after Janie and I were married about "becoming one." When I wrote this, I never dreamed that it would be included in a book.

"Today Janie and I have been married for forty-five years. When I made my 'until dead do us part' vow back then, I had no idea what I was talking about. Hey, after all, I was just nineteen. I only knew that in that moment I wanted Janie (officially the Prettiest Girl I Ever Saw) by my side to share my life, to be my love.

"Well, after forty-five years I now think I have a better appreciation for what 'until death do us part' really means. Through the years, in the good times and bad, in the rich times and in the poor, in the blessed times and, yes, even in that rare and crazy time long ago when we just wanted to throw our hands up and quit, God has woven our lives together into a bond that truly can only be broken by death.

"It was a bond that did not happen all it once. Rather, it was a journey of sharing and commitment and passion and perseverance. It was a journey of soft love and tough love-what I call Pit Bull Love-a love that never even considers failure as an option. And it was a journey of little things, day-to-day things, the mundane things mixed in with the exciting things that God used to transform 'me and thee' into 'we.'

"As I get older and reflect on that journey, I cannot imagine what life would have been like without Janie. God gave me exactly the partner I needed."

Now, if I may, I have only one small bit of parting advice I can give to you. Go now. Find two cups of coffee. Go find your partner. Now, sit down and start talking. Talk about what, you ask? Anything. Anything at all. Just start talking. You may be surprised by the results.